Rockett's World

ARE WE THERE YET?

Read more about

Rockett's World

in:

#1 WHO CAN YOU TRUST?

#2 WHAT KIND OF FRIEND ARE YOU?

Purple Moon

Rockett's World

ARE WE THERE YET?

Lauren Day

Waldorf School of Pittsburgh Library

SCHOLASTIC INC.

New York Toronto London Auckland Sydney
Mexico City New Delhi Hong Kong

ISBN 0-439-08209-9

12 11 10 9 8 7 6 5 4 3 2 1   9/9 0 1 2 3 4/0

Printed in the U.S.A.   40
First Scholastic printing, November 1999

Rockett's World

ARE WE THERE YET?

INTRODUCTION

When I first got to Whistling Pines Junior High School a few months ago, everyone said, "This is the coolest school on the planet." Back then I wasn't so sure. I felt beige in a plaid world. But now? Color me a believer. I am mega-psyched to be here! I've made so many friends. A lot of kids are majorly awesome; others are, well, let's just say *complicated*.

Take Jessie Marbella, for instance. We're not *best* friends, but she's this totally sweet girl I've gotten to know pretty well. Okay, a little oversensitive sometimes, but I know I can trust her with secrets and stuff. The thing is, Jessie is tighter with this other girl, Darnetta James, who I haven't exactly bonded with. I would be better friends with Jessie if not for Darnetta. I *think*.

Then there's Miko Kajiyama and Nakili Abuto. We met in art class and totally connected. But there's a little complication there, too! Along with another girl, Dana St. Clair (who *doesn't* like me!), they're in the CSGs. That's a sorta secret club since most people don't know CSG stands for "Cool Sagittarius Girls." I'm not in the club, but at least they're not snobby.

That title is totally reserved for The Ones. Can you believe they actually named themselves that?! The main members are Nicole Whittaker, Stephanie Hollis, and Whitney Weiss. The funny thing is, I actually *like* Whitney, and Steph can be sweet — but Nicole! I've learned the hard way to watch out for her.

Just a few weeks ago, we had our student elections. I ran for secretary on the CSG team, but The Ones beat us. Now Nicole is class president, and Whitney, Stephanie, and Cleve Goodstaff are officers.

Um, did I mention the boys at WP? They're pretty interesting, too — especially this one boy, the absolute coolest of all, Ruben Rosales. He plays guitar and isn't part of any clique. That's the way I want to be: a person who makes friends with people for who they are, not what clique they belong to.

Right now, I am beyond psyched. Our class trip is coming up. Because they're class officers, The Ones got to choose the destination. For once, they did something cool — they chose an overnight (!!) to Chicago (!! — never been, can't wait to go!!). Better of all (can you say that?), an entire day is set aside just for this famous art museum. Best of all, *everyone*'s totally going! This is going to be my best time ever at Whistling Pines — I feel it in my bones.

CHAPTER ONE

"Whoo-*hoo*! Look at that — sign-ups for the class trip start today! Can't wait to go!" Joyfully, Rockett Movado pointed to a brand-new poster tacked up on the hallway wall.

In block letters shaded by pastels, it read: EIGHTH-GRADE CLASS TRIP — BE THERE OR BE NOWHERE!!! COME ONE, COME ALL TO THE ART INSTITUTE OF CHICAGO, A WEEKEND TRIP TO ROCK YOUR WORLD — SIGN UP NOW!

It was just before lunch period, and the three girls Rockett was walking with stopped to eyeball the poster. Each had a different reaction to it.

Nakili Abuto flashed her trademark megawatt smile. "All *right*, girlfriends, straight from lunch, let's do the sign-up thing. I'm all over a new adventure!"

Neatly dressed Miko Kajiyama squinted behind her wingtip glasses and whipped a small notebook out of her backpack. "Me too — I'm starting my list of what to pack now. I totally don't want to forget anything."

Only the third girl, Dana St. Clair, tall and angular with fiery red hair, made a face. Hand on hip, she struck a pose and groused, "Would you just look at that!" She pointed to the words on the bottom of the poster, snick-

3

ering. BROUGHT TO YOU BY YOUR ELECTED OFFICIALS, THE
ONES PARTY: NICOLE, CLEVE, STEPHANIE, AND WHITNEY.

Confused, Miko wondered aloud, "What's your problem?"

"That is *so* like them," Dana huffed, "taking full credit for our class trip! They are beyond self-congratulatory. As if they thought of it all by themselves."

Grinning good-naturedly, Nakili reminded her, "Reality check, girlfriend, they *did*."

"Well, I totally don't *want* to give them credit, but you have to admit, they own this one," Miko concurred.

"Puh-*leeze*," Dana countered, dismissing her. "The only thing they 'own' is their snobby 'tudes and the inborn ability to steal other people's ideas and pretend they thought of them themselves. Remember in that class . . . when they did that thing . . . in that place?"

Rockett had no idea what Dana was referring to.

But Miko and Nakili did. "That was a year ago," Miko pointed out. "You totally can't compare."

"That was whack," Nakili agreed. "This time it's different. . . ."

Rocket watched as Nakili, Miko, and Dana — the CSGs, as they called themselves — formed a circle and bantered. They'd been friends for so long, they had their own shorthand bickering rhythm. She marveled at it — even as her own feelings took a nosedive. Just a few weeks ago, she'd been on their team, running for student council *with* them. And one second ago, as she'd walked between fourth-period science and fifth-period lunch,

4

she'd felt part of their group. Now she was back on the outside, looking in. Had they meant to do that?

This is ridiculous! I mean, I've become really tight with them. I should just say, 'Hey, guys, remember me? I'm still here! And I'm needing a back story. But . . . what if they think that's lame? I should just stand here until they finish talking about The Ones — how much more is there to say, anyway? Oh, you know what? Forget it. I'll just slink away. But what if they don't even notice I'm gone? How pathetic would that make me feel?

Screwing up her courage, Rockett took a small but deliberate step closer to their little circle. She interjected, "C'mon, guys, who cares who thought up the idea for the trip? The big picture is, we're *going*! How cool is that?"

Instantly, Miko whirled around and stepped back to include Rockett. Shaking her head in agreement, she noted, "Rockett's right. Besides, it was the only one of their campaign promises they managed to make good on."

"The only one that was worthy," Rockett reminded her friends. "The rest were so superficial."

And didn't she know it. Before Rockett had chosen to be part of the CSGs' team to run for class elections, Nicole (for her own devious reasons) had actually invited her to be part of The Ones ticket — as vice president! So Rockett knew all about their campaign promises — how The Ones vowed to change the rules so kids could carry cell phones, wear flip-flops, and have no homework on Fridays.

Nakili reminded Rockett, "They got the thumbs-down by the teachers on all that stuff. They promised everything, but they got nothing."

"Yeah, right," Dana said sarcastically. "The only thing *they* got was . . . elected. Unlike us. *We* deserved to win. We could have made good on all our campaign pledges."

Miko chided, "Sour grapes is totally unproductive. We just have to work within the system to make the school better, that's all."

Before Dana could retort — though Rockett was pretty sure she saw the words *Goody Two-shoes* forming on her lips, a new voice spoke up.

Laced with boredom, a girl said, "Get over it, St. Clair. You lost. Typical." Sharla Norvell, all spiky hair, thick black eye liner, leather jacket, and perpetual sneer, was brushing by them.

Dana whipped around — geared up and combat ready. "We may have lost the election, Sharla, but you're the one walking around Whistling Pines with a huge O — for *outcast* — on your back. And everyone knows it."

Sharla stopped in her tracks and peered threateningly at Dana. "You got a problem, St. Clair? We can settle this after school — out back. Just you and me. Alone."

Dana shrank a little. "That *would* be your solution," she mumbled, turning back to her friends.

Sharla retorted, "Thought so. You're only tough with your mouth — and with your friends around. Typical." With that, she skulked away.

Rockett was aghast, not only at the heated exchange,

6

but mostly at Dana. Indignantly, she demanded, "How could you say that to her? Even if you don't like her — or are scared of her or something — Sharla voted for us, you know."

Dana scoffed. "Big help that was, Rockett. You reeled in a huge vote there."

Nakili yanked Dana's arm and aimed her toward the lunchroom. "Come on, let's jet to the caf. Don't wanna miss out in case there's something remotely edible today."

On cue, Miko tried to guide Rockett in the other direction. "Let's confirm our attendance on the class trip first," she said. "We'll meet up in the lunchroom."

Dana allowed herself to be diverted by Nakili, but not without getting the last word in. "Who's afraid of the big bad Sharla, anyway? Not me."

As if that wasn't enough, to Miko she added, "Why don't you come with us? Rockett probably wants to go catch up with her NBF anyway."

Defensive, Rockett snapped, "Just because I talked to Sharla doesn't make her my 'new best friend.' And just because you don't like her doesn't give you the right to diss her like that. Get a grip, will you?"

But Dana — half *dragged* by Nakili now — was already halfway down the hall.

Shaking her head, Rockett gently removed Miko's hand from her elbow. She took a deep breath to calm down. "It's okay, Miko. Go with them. I have to do a pit stop in the girls' room. We can do the class trip thing after eighth period."

Miko frowned. "Are you sure? I mean . . ."

"Really, I'm fine. Anyway, look at this. The pen I was using last period must have leaked all over my hands. I have to wash up."

Miko tilted her head, obviously not convinced that Dana hadn't hurt Rockett's feelings. "I'll wait for you," she said. "Then we can check off our names on the class trip list and get to the lunchroom in plenty of time. Why don't you sit with us today, anyway?"

I probably should. There's got to be some good in Dana if the two of them are friends with her. Maybe if I just stick it out and show her she can't get to me, it'll work out. But wait. Except for a few minutes during the campaign, she still treats me like dirt. Just like she treats certain other people, too. No, Dana should apologize to me! I should just leave things as they are and sit at my usual table. I guess.

Confession Session

I've had it up to here with Dana's insecurity! I love that girl like a sista-friend, but she's getting ridiculous with her anti-Rockett tirades. I'm gonna end this once and for all. I'm gonna make a motion that even though Rockett's not technically a Sagittarius, we ask her to join the CSGs. She just fits in with us. And Dana's just gonna have to deal.

I'm so totally disappointed! During the election campaign, Dana and Rockett were really getting along. When we were all aligned for one purpose. And now that we lost, it's like they're back to square one. I wish Dana wasn't so threatened by Rockett. It's not like we have to choose between them.

CHAPTER TWO

Rockett smiled at Miko. "That's so sweet of you, but you don't have to make up for Dana's obnoxious personality. I'll be at the table next to you, like always. With Jessie, Darnetta, and Mavis." Rockett wished she sounded more enthusiastic about her lunch buds. They were, she reminded herself, her friends — mostly.

"Okay, see you there, but if you change your mind you're always welcome. Today or any other day," Miko assured her. "And Rockett? Let's try to room together on the overnight to Chicago, okay?"

"Absolutely!" Rockett replied, heading off toward the girls' room. Just thinking about the upcoming overnight was all it took to set Rockett back on course: Her sunny-side-up nature resurfaced. Photography was her number-one interest in life. Getting to go to a famous museum with an amazing photo gallery, *with* all her friends — without parents, or her annoying brother — was going to be beyond awesome.

A few minutes later, Rockett pushed open the door to the girls' room. She heard two distinct sounds. One was the high-pitched chatter of the three girls crowded around the middle sink. Nicole Whittaker, Whitney

Weiss, and Stephanie Hollis, the core of The Ones, were doing mirror-time, applying their makeup and fixing their hair.

The other sound, which came from inside one of the three stalls, sounded like someone trying to muffle her sobs. Rockett would have turned her full attention to the latter, but one of the girls at the mirror was instantly all over her.

"Hey, Rockett, s'up? Did you even *get* that science assignment — I mean who cares about plates beneath the earth's surface? Is it a science teacher mission to dig up the most boring stuff and force us to memorize it?" Chatty, curly-haired Whitney was the only girl in The Ones crowd that Rockett had gotten sorta friendly with. And she *always* had issues with her schoolwork!

But before she could respond, tall, sleek Nicole slyly inserted, "Be careful talking to her about assignments, she might think you're trying to cheat again."

Sore-subject alert! Whitney turned on Nicole. "How *new*! Don't you ever let *anything* go? The rest of the world did, like, weeks ago."

By now, Rockett knew not to fall into Nicole's trap. She changed the subject quickly. "So I was looking at the posters you guys put up for the class trip. I'm psyched! I've never been to Chicago. Have you?"

Although she'd been talking to Whitney, Nicole sniffed, "Dozens of times."

Leave it to the snob-princess to claim bragging rights.

12

Nicole continued, "There's only one huge problem — so many designer boutiques, so little time!"

That is so her! Like shopping is the whole reason we're going. She is so superficial!

Stephanie added, "We'll just have to stake out the most beautiful boutiques and plan a route. . . ." Rockett tuned out. Just then, a door to one of the stalls creaked open. Rockett spun around to see who it was — and if that person had possibly been crying.

Mavis Wartella-Depew, her hair even more askew than normal, emerged and headed for the sinks. She made eye contact with no one.

It wasn't just her weird name that made Mavis different. It was the combination of her personality and her offbeat looks that separated her from the other kids at Whistling Pines. The short, boxy girl with the square glasses actually believed she was psychic and could predict the future.

Other kids made fun of her, but Rockett was determined not to. She didn't exactly want to be best friends with Mavis, but she did find her kind of interesting.

"Hey, Mavis," Rockett started, separating herself from The Ones and walking over to where Mavis was washing up. "Did you brown-bag it today, or are you risking the cafeteria excuse-for-food?"

Mavis's eyes were trained on the faucets, so Rockett couldn't really see if they were red.

With a dismissive shake of her head, she said, "I'm

not going to lunch today, Rockett. I have . . . a . . . kind of . . . something else to do this period." Without a backward glance, Mavis shot out the door.

That's weird. She's acting totally un-Mavis. Almost like she's brushing me off! I don't get it.

"What a break for you," Nicole sniffed. "Only three geeks at your table today, instead of the usual dork-tet."

Rockett would have laced into Nicole, but Darnetta James, just emerging from the second stall, did it for her. "Watch who you're calling a geek, you snob-freak." She punctuated this with a seamless slam of the stall door.

Well, she's not the mystery sobber.

Nicole snapped her blush case shut and tossed it into her bag. "While this . . . encounter . . . has been soooo enlightening, buh-*bye*, elsewhere to be!" With that, she — trailed by Whitney and Stephanie — flounced out the door.

"You go," Rockett said to Darnetta admiringly. "You really gave it back."

Darnetta threw her head back. "A diss a day chases The Ones away."

Rockett dropped her backpack on the floor, ready to soap her inky hands. "I don't know why they're always so evil. And sometimes," she added, "I think Dana's a secret One — she fits the profile."

"That's why I don't get too deep into the cliques and all that," Darnetta responded, swiping a scratchy napkin from the dispenser to dry her hands. "Who needs it? I do my thing, and I have my friends, that's enough." She tossed the wipe into the trash bin and added, "Jessie's saving a place for me in line. Want us to hold one for you?"

"No, that's all right. It's gonna take me a few minutes to get this ink off my hands." While Rockett admitted it was a sweet gesture to include her, she still felt like a third wheel when it came to Jessie and Darnetta. But that wasn't the only reason she told Darnetta to go on ahead. She was really curious now to find out who else was in the girls' room — and might be crying. It *could* have been Mavis — but that would be *so* out of character.

She didn't have long to wait. As she scrubbed her hands, the third door slowly creaked open. Rockett meant to glance up in the mirror casually to see who it was, but her own reflection betrayed her: Her look was anything but casual.

Sharla.

Rockett's radar went off. The eye makeup that had been thick but smooth a few minutes ago seemed smudged now. If Rockett was right, that could only mean one thing: Tough-girl Sharla had been crying! *I bet she was really stung by Dana! Oh! I know just how she feels. What can I say that will make her feel better — and won't wound her pride?*

The best Rockett could come up with was: "That Dana. She's been nothing but snarky to me, too, since I got here. What's her saga, anyway?"

Sharla might have had an opinion, but Rockett would

never know. For Sharla chose silence. Clutching her books to her chest, without even bothering to repair her makeup, she left the room in a hurry.

I didn't handle that one too well. I just hope I didn't make her feel any worse. How choice would that be?

Rockett crouched to pick up her backpack. That's when, out of the corner of her eye, she noticed something on the floor. A note, folded up origami style. Sure it hadn't been there when she first walked into the girls' room, she picked it up.

One of them must have dropped it! But who? It could be Nicole, Whitney, Stephanie, Mavis, Darnetta, or Sharla. I should just go over to each one and ask whose it is. But what if it's Darnetta's or Sharla's — and Nicole grabs it and pretends it's hers or something? That would be just like her! Or I could try to find Darnetta and Mavis first — but I have no idea where Mavis went. Maybe I should just open it a crack to see who signed it. I wouldn't even read it. Then its rightful owner will get it back, without being made fun of or anything. Or I could just leave it here. Whoever lost it will realize it soon enough and come back for it.

CHAPTER THREE

Time elapsed deliberating? Half a second. To be sure no one caught her, Rockett slipped into a stall and slid the lock closed. She carefully opened the note.

Dear Nigel,
    The class trip — what a rip! It's not 4me, can't go that low, ain't got no dough. So leave me here, leave me out . . . to dry.

Rockett's eyes widened as she got to the last word. *Typical.*

She knew exactly who the author was. And exactly what she had to do.

Sticking the note inside her science book, Rockett raced out of the girls' room and made it to the lunchroom in record time. The place was jam-packed with students. Most had already gone through the line and were now balancing lunch trays, bellowing to be heard above the din. She noticed a couple of boys doing yo-yo tricks at one table; others were playing with handheld video games.

A few people greeted her as she zigzagged through the

room — but Rockett didn't stop to talk. After eyeballing the lunch line, she snaked her way around the tables until she found the one person she needed to talk to. Jessie Marbella was the girl Rockett could *totally* trust with this highly confidential 411 — and she also gave great advice.

Jessie, wearing a purple T-shirt and butterfly choker beads, was already seated at their usual table. Next to her, of course, was Darnetta. The two were poring over a textbook, scarfing their sandwiches.

Coming up behind them, Rockett tapped Jessie on the shoulder. "Can I talk to you?"

Jessie spun around and shot Rockett a huge smile. "Hey, you didn't even get in line yet? You better hurry, there's not much left."

"I'm . . . uh . . . I'll eat later. Look, could you come with me for a sec?" Uncomfortably, Rockett realized that she was ignoring Darnetta. How rude was that? But what she had to share was for Jessie's ears only. If you told one person, it was a confidence. More than one, it was gossip.

Then Rockett added, "Excuse us, okay, Darnetta?"

Jessie's conflicted feelings were like a road map all over her face. Biting her lip, she went, "'Netta and I were just in the middle of quizzing each other for the math test. Is this some kind of emergency or something?"

"Yeah! I mean . . . not exactly . . . but it'll only take a minute . . ." she totally sputtered. For the second time that day, Darnetta bailed her out. "Go on, Jessie. I've got to get with my language arts homework the rest of this period anyway. I'll catch you next class."

Warily, Jessie asked, "Are you sure?"

"Emphatically. Just go."

Still conflicted, Jessie scooped up her sandwich and her iced tea and followed Rockett out of the lunchroom.

"Let's go outside," Rockett suggested as they headed down the corridor. "This time of the day, it's pretty empty. We can talk privately."

"This must be top secret stuff," Jessie guessed, "shared only on a need-to-know basis, huh?"

Rockett pushed open the door that led to the front of the school. "I accidentally found something out about someone. It's kind of embarrassing. And I don't want to make it any worse for that person."

"So what *do* you want to do?" Jessie asked, following her outside, curious now.

"I want to help — and I want your advice. You're always so good at this, and I completely trust you."

For the first time since Rockett interrupted her lunch, Jessie smiled. "You're right — I mean, it's deserted out here, everyone's in the cafeteria."

Rockett led Jessie to an empty bench. Sitting down, she pulled her notebook out of her backpack and opened it to where she'd stashed the note.

Intrigued, Jessie glanced at it. "All right, Rockett — you've got my total attention. Spill!"

Rockett took a deep breath. "Okay, here's the thing. I was just in the girls' room — The Ones were there, and so were Darnetta and Mavis. And Sharla. I was the last one to leave. I found this on the floor." She handed the note to Jessie.

Jessie arched her eyebrows. "You read someone else's private note? I'm . . . I guess . . . surprised."

Rockett flushed. "I wasn't sure if I should. But I just didn't want to leave it on the floor — you know, what if it was supersensitive and fell into the wrong hands? And I was totally going to return it, but I . . . I don't know, I was curious, I guess. Anyway, when you read it, you'll see I did the right thing. At the risk of channeling Mavis — who knows, maybe it was fate or something that made me find it."

"There's only one way to find out," her friend finally agreed. As Jessie read the note, her eyes widened. Handing it back to Rockett, she ventured, "Wow. This is huge. And soooo sad! You think you know who wrote this?"

"I'm *sure* I do. It definitely was *not* written by any of The Ones. It isn't Mavis's style. . . ."

"And it sure isn't 'Netta's," Jessie-the-Darnetta-expert said.

"Which leaves . . ."

Rockett and Jessie exchanged knowing looks. Jessie pursed her lips and mused, "You could be right. This is exactly the kind of poetry Sharla would write — if Sharla wrote poetry, that is. Who knows?"

"That's just it," Rockett exclaimed. "No one knows that much about her — period. But now we know this —

unlike just about *everyone* else in the entire eighth grade, *she* doesn't want to go on the class trip."

Jessie turned the note over and stared into the distance. "Do you think it's because, uh, no one's friends with her?"

Rocket considered. "Maybe."

"But . . ." Jessie suddenly snapped back and looked straight at Rockett. "I've been in the same school as her since elementary. And she's never cared about having friends. Not ever."

Rockett said gently, "There's more. She was crying."

Just then — in a bad-timing moment of colossal proportions — the school door banged open. Two very familiar, and very loud, boys blasted through. One was dressed in a prep-perfect button-down, long-sleeved shirt, neatly tucked into his chinos; the other, his polar opposite, wore a T-shirt outside his baggy jeans.

Jessie spun around and immediately reddened. "It's Max!" She blurted, "What's he doing with Ruben?"

Max Diamond, cocky, confident smart aleck, was a full-fledged member of The Ones. Normally, he hung out with his cocky, confident "other half," the athletic Cleve Goodstaff. Or with another of The Ones, like diplomatic Chaz Franklin. He was hardly ever with indie-boy Ruben.

Rockett and Jessie didn't have to ponder long about why this unlikely duo was together — they were obviously in the middle of a fierce yo-yo challenge. Rockett figured they'd probably been disrupting the cafeteria and were told by one of the aides to "take it outside, gentlemen."

Ruben, his back now to the girls, was flinging his yo-yo in Max's face and taunting, "Amateur! No way is that Around the World. That's whack."

Max had just started to demonstrate. "Is so! I'll show you how it's . . ."

Max stopped midsentence, spying Jessie and Rockett. "Hey . . ." he stammered.

Rockett didn't notice Jessie blushing, nor did she pick up on the usually confident Max's sudden loss for a glib greeting. Ruben did, though. He spun around to see what had distracted Max from their competition.

Focusing on Rockett, Ruben waved. "Hey, new girl!"

Ruben always greeted Rockett that way — probably always would, she thought.

"Hey yourself," Rockett replied as coolly as she could.

Ruben and Max took that as an invitation to join the girls — not that it was! — and scampered over. In a split second, the boys were close enough to see Jessie fiddling with the note and Rockett starting to look alarmed.

"Wassup, ladies — passing notes outside of school? Or is one of you helping the other to compose a love letter?" That was Ruben's idea of a tease. At any other moment, Rockett would have been cool with it, might even have swapped one-ups with him — but this so wasn't the time.

"Um, Ruben . . . uh, later? We're kind of in the middle of something important." *And how lame do I feel saying that — even though it's true?*

Before Ruben could respond, Max clutched his heart in mock tragedy. "She doesn't want to talk to you. Dude, she's blowing you off."

If Rockett had been paying more attention, she would have seen the glances exchanged between Jessie and Max, but all she noticed were Ruben's mischievous twinkling eyes.

"Okay, new girl, I can take a hint. We're gone."

When they finally were, Rockett turned back to Jessie. Her friend's eyes darted to the ground. That's when Rockett remembered something. Wasn't it only a few weeks back that Max had given Jessie a gift — anonymously, pretending to be a secret admirer? But eventually Jessie found out who it was. And now they were sort of circling each other. Not saying anything to anyone, not even to each other.

"Oops, my bad," Rocket apologized. "Did you want to hang out with Max?"

A little too emphatically, Jessie exclaimed, "No way! I mean, not now."

Rockett didn't believe her, but decided not to push. They'd come outside for a reason, and lunch period was almost over. "So, about what I was saying," she started.

Jessie picked up the convo. "Right. Sharla was really crying? I can't even picture it. But you saw her?"

"Not exactly," Rockett admitted. "I mean, she was in

23

one of the stalls, and when she came out, her makeup was all smudged. And I've ruled out the other two. It had to be her."

"That's bad. I bet she'd kill you if she knew you knew — worse, that you told someone."

Rockett shuddered, remembering Sharla's challenge to Dana. "Well, I'm obviously not gonna tell her — right? But I can't help feeling bad that she won't go on the trip."

"That's sweet of you, but she obviously doesn't want to go. She doesn't like any of us. Why should you care?"

"I guess I wouldn't, if I thought that was really it. But give me the note . . ."

Jessie did.

"Look at this line here." Rockett pointed to the line *ain't got no dough*. "I think she can't afford to go."

Jessie shook her head. "That can't be it. The money comes out of a school fund. That's how every trip is run at Whistling Pines."

Rockett mused, "So the kids, or the parents, don't contribute *anything*?"

"Well, just extras and stuff . . ." Jessie trailed off, biting her lip. "I mean, you're not supposed to have to need extra money. But everyone brings it. Everyone buys souvenirs and stuff. Some more than others, of course."

"Has Sharla gone on any class trips that you remember?"

Jessie thought for a moment. "Back in sixth grade . . . uh, now that you mention it, I just realized. It was horri-

24

ble. I mean, it was just a day trip to this arboretum. And Sharla sat by herself and ate her brown-bag lunch, when everyone else got to buy snacks and souvenirs and stuff. No one said anything. It was weird."

"I rest my case," Rockett concluded. "What are we going to do about it?"

"We?"

"Come on, Jessie — she's . . . I mean, she could be a good person deep down. She voted for the CSGs in the student elections, you know. Anyway, the trip is supposed to be for everyone. Not just for people with extra money."

Jessie shrugged. "I don't know. I guess we could take up a collection or something."

"How totally humiliating would that be? There's got to be a better idea."

At that moment, the bell rang, signaling the end of the period. Jessie gathered her books and stood up. She took a deep breath and looked down at Rockett, still perched on the bench. "Here's what I think, Rockett. You've got three choices. One: Just let it go. In my experience, getting involved in other people's private stuff never works out. Or two — and this is only if you *can't* butt out — ask Mr. Baldus for input. He's one of the chaperones."

Rockett considered. "What's number three?"

Jessie folded her arms across her chest. "*This* is crucial. Talk to Sharla first. The note sounds totally obvious — but what if you're wrong . . . about everything?"

Jessie's right. I should probably forget the whole thing. It's not my business. But how can I? I feel soooo bad for Sharla! I'll just go to Baldus and get advice. But . . . should I, like, talk to Sharla and make sure I'm right? No — I know I'm right. Of course Sharla wrote the note. But how can I approach her about it? She'd know I read it. She'd go ballistic!

Confession Session

Rockett always does this to me! She knows it makes me feel good that I'm the only person she confides in. But it makes me feel bad at the same time. I don't feel right knowing stuff about other people that they don't want you to know.

CHAPTER FOUR

"Welcome to my one-and-only-no-baloney eighth-grade home-a-room-a-roney!" Mr. Baldus bellowed the next morning. With Baldus, you never knew what cliché he was going to greet the class with — just that it was going to be over the top on the cheese-o-meter.

Today, Rockett knew something no one else did: exactly what Baldus was going to talk about after he took attendance. For she *had* gone to seek his advice about the letter — without telling Sharla, or anyone besides Jessie.

Well, not exactly anyone.

On her way to Baldus's room yesterday afternoon, Rockett had bumped into Mavis. The self-proclaimed psychic still seemed . . . off somehow. Impulsively, Rockett had touched her elbow. "Are you all right?"

Almost defensively, Mavis had countered, "Do I not look all *right* to you, Rockett?"

"You seem distracted or something."

Mavis had shifted her eyes uncomfortably and mumbled, "Did you want something?"

No way had Rockett planned to tell Mavis this, but for some reason she just blurted, "I kinda think there might be some people in our grade who aren't going on the class trip because they don't have the extra spending money. I'm going to talk to Mr. Baldus about it." Rockett nodded toward his office, a few doors down. "Come with me?"

Rocket was sure Mavis would want to — or least be complimented that she'd been invited.

Wrong. For instead, Mavis had scowled, crinkling her forehead. "How do you even know this, Rockett? And even if you're right, what makes it your business?"

Strange encounters of the Mavis kind! Normally, she'd be psyched to be included. And most of the time, she goes out of her way to help me. I wonder what's up with her? Oh, well, one crisis at a time.

At least Baldus had reacted the way Rockett hoped. He didn't ask *how* she knew who was stuck for bucks: Instead, he figured out what to do. And now he was about to inform the class.

On the blackboard, he wrote in huge block letters: CLASS TRIP FUND-RAISER. He underlined it twice before spinning around to face the class. "As everyone knows, our can't-be-beat, no-retreat class trip to Chicago is creeping up. And I've got a super-duper-scooper to lay on ya. Ready? Incoming: New year, new rule. Every student starts the trip with the same amount of spending money. This eliminates the need for allowance-dipping or hitting up the 'rents for the moolah. 'Cause the dough's gonna rise right here — heh, heh — in the next two weeks. Got it?"

Judging by the twenty pairs of eyes staring widely at him, the answer to that question was a resounding "Huh?"

30

Cleve's hand slowly went up. He brushed a wayward shock of blond hair out of his eyes and went, "Why?"

Mr. Baldus replied, "Ah, but yours is not to question why, Mr. Goodstaff, yours is but to listen and try . . . to come up with a boss money-making idea — fast! 'Cause here's the grooviest part of all. My most inventive class — this means you! — gets to brainstorm and decide on the fund-raiser."

Whitney frantically waved her hand. "Who thought of this dumb idea? I mean, no one even asked us about this! And we represent the voice of the students. . . ."

Baldus sighed. "Your point, Ms. Weiss?"

Whitney rolled her eyes. "What's wrong with the old way of doing it? We bring what we want. It makes no sense that everyone in our entire class is going to be given spending money for the trip."

Mr. Baldus answered, "Not *given*. You creative brainiacs are going to raise the roof to raise the dough, so everyone's on the same spending wagon. It's so democratic I can't believe we never thought of this before!"

Nicole uncoiled. She actually stood up. "Be kind. Rewind," she purred. "Are you saying what I think you're saying? That everyone is going to be given the same amount of spending money — and everyone *has* to spend the same amount? That I *can't* spend more if I want to?"

Mr. Baldus was hardly ever in a bad mood. But Cleve, Whitney, and now Nicole were definitely pushing him. With a forced smile, through clenched teeth he said, "Take your seat, Ms. Whittaker. Let's be clear. This is a no-vote situation. It's a done deal. So let's come up with a quick 'n' easy plan to raise that stash-o-class-trip cash! The suggestion with the most votes wins, and" — he paused, making it seem as if he just thought it up — "because Rockett Movado is one of our ace yearbook shutterbugs, I hereby appoint her to head up the effort on behalf of the winning idea!"

Oh, no, why did he do that? Now everyone will guess that I had something to do with this!

Rockett tried to act as though she were as appalled at the idea as everyone else seemed to be. She stole a glance at Sharla, but the girl's face was a stony blank slate.

Baldus expertly maneuvered the class's attention back to where he wanted it. Although he had to keep them way past the bell for first period, he eventually did get some people to start coming up with fund-raising ideas.

Miko got with the program first. "In my sister's school, they had a bake sale. We could do that."

Over a few random, rude, "That is so lame" protests, Baldus wrote on the blackboard: NUMBER 1: BAKE SALE.

He turned to Miko. "That's the spirit! A mouthwatering start. Who else has an idea?"

Once Miko broke the ice, Dana dived in. "What about a student-teacher soccer game that we could sell tickets to?"

Rockett wondered if Dana was just being supportive of her sister CSG — so it wouldn't look like Miko was the only one going alone with Baldus — or if she really was into the fund-raiser. Whichever, Rockett had to give her props.

Dana boasted, "We'd blast the teachers away."

Baldus lit up. "My shins are aching already! Good one, Dana." He put that idea down for Number 2.

Nakili was next. "We could pick up cans and newspapers and recycle them for cash — that way we raise money and do some environmental good."

Baldus was acting like this was the best day of his life. And for that — and for *not* giving away the real reason for the fund-raiser — he just entered Rockett's personal All-Star Teachers hall of fame.

"We've hit the trifecta: three stellar suggestions," he announced. "Do I hear a fourth? If not, we'll vote on these. Going, going . . ."

Stephanie's hand shot up. "What about a track race? Boys against girls. There'd be no contest who would win."

"Ha! We'll kill you." Cleve jumped in with a knee-jerk reaction, his athletic skills suddenly questioned.

"I'd pay to see that." Ruben laughed, slapping the desk for emphasis.

"And that, kiddies, is what the whole thing's about," Mr. Baldus, beaming now, reminded them as he wrote Stephanie's suggestion on the board.

And just like that, the class did a total 180: Each tried to top the other with an idea. As if they forgot how *versus* they'd been only moments ago.

Arrow Mayfield, a musician who fronted her own student band, suggested an in-line skate-a-thon. "Not for competition, just for fun. We could wear shirts from local businesses, who'd sponsor it."

Then gawky Arnold Zeitbaum weighed in. Obsessed with all things retro — *really* retro, like from the Middle Ages — he gushed, "A duel! We'll dress up as knights and duel like they did in medieval times. All the peasants will pay to see it."

It didn't surprise Rockett that most of the class dissed Arnold's suggestion. Neither he, nor his ideas, were very popular.

Next Jessie spoke up. "I saw this on a TV show," she ventured. "How about a calendar for next year that we make ourselves? Twelve of us could volunteer to pose. And then parents and teachers and other people we know would pledge to buy it."

The expression on Nicole's face suddenly morphed from bored to floored. Bouncing out of her seat, she exclaimed, "That's it! I just thought of it! We'll call it 'The Cool Kids of Whistling Pines Calendar'! The most camera-friendly of us will pose. Am I a genius or what?"

Rockett was appalled. The nerve of her — taking Jessie's idea, twisting it to include only "cool" kids — and then actually saying "*I* just thought of it"? Rockett whirled around. Eyes flashing, she urged Jessie to speak up.

But her sweet friend would not. Rockett was just about to, but it was too late. The Ones instantly rallied behind what had now become Nicole's idea, while other kids like Nakili, Dana, Miko, Ruben, and Arrow registered a loud vote against it. Mr. Baldus rapped the pointer on the blackboard to bring order back to the class.

Not that he was upset. Just the opposite: He was pumped. "Okeydokey — I tell you, there's no class like this one when it comes to creativity! We'll vote by silent ballot, and at the end of the day I'll announce the winning idea! Come with me now to Recapville: Here are the suggestions for the class trip fund-raiser. Bake sale, student-teacher soccer game, boys-against-girls track race, recycling, in-line skate-a-palooza, medieval duel, and student calendar."

Just before dismissing them, he instructed, "Discuss amongst yourselves how to pull this off in two weeks, and which suggestion will raise the most moolah!"

The surprise fund-raiser was the big topic of conversation throughout Whistling Pines that day. Except for a few holdouts who refused to be drawn into it — brooding, quiet Wolf DuBois, outsider-boy Bo Pezanski, and of course Sharla — it was like the class elections all over again. Everyone tried to rally support for the idea he or she liked best. And like always, Rockett noted, kids lined up with their friends.

Because they thought it would make the most money, Nakili, Miko, and Dana all decided to vote for Dana's suggestion, the teacher-student soccer game. In art class, they tried to convince Rockett to do the same. "This is so fly," Nakili had said exuberantly. "The whole town will pay to come see it — all the kids at Whistling Pines, the high school kids who remember their teachers, all the parents, everyone. It'll raise the most money."

Rockett had to agree. The thought of seeing the teachers in soccer gear had to be a huge draw. She wouldn't miss it!

Others could, though. Just as she feared, during math class Arnold sidled up to her and talked up his medieval knight duel. "Sports competitions, calendars, bake sales, begone!" he declared with a customary flourish. "Don't go with the crowd, Rockett, be a bold one!"

"It sounds . . . really different, Arnold," Rockett said carefully, not wanting to hurt his feelings. "I'll definitely consider it."

Satisfied, Arnold smiled, did this little half-bow thing that embarrassed Rockett, and walked back to his desk happy.

Whew! I managed to tell the truth and not hurt his feelings. Success!

The Ones — Nicole, Stephanie, Whitney, Cleve, Max, and Chaz — were all over "their" calendar idea. By lunch, they'd even sketched out drawings for the design.

In the cafeteria, when Rockett sat down next to Jessie, she finally exploded. "Aren't you ballistic they stole your idea? Why didn't you say anything in homeroom?"

Jessie shrugged. "That's so them. Anyway, who cares who thought of it, as long as it wins?"

36

Although Rockett had said practically the same thing to Dana about the class trip, this time she was really annoyed. She turned to Darnetta for support. "Don't you think she should be mad?"

Darnetta took a bite of her sandwich before answering. Then she shrugged. "Jessie's just not territorial the way some people are. She's about what's fun, what makes sense, not about who takes credit."

So Darnetta's saying I'm territorial? I just don't get her, and I'm beginning to see why I never will.

Rockett turned back to Jessie. "So I guess that means you two are voting for the calendar idea?"

Jessie pointed out, "If it wins, they'd need a photographer. And since you and 'Netta are on the yearbook photo staff, you could both do it. Besides, didn't Baldus put you in charge of the whole thing? You could even design it."

Truthfully? Rockett hadn't considered that. Now she couldn't help being stoked. "I guess. I mean, that *would* be amazing."

"Check it, here's *my* question," Darnetta said, interrupting them. "What's up with this sudden Baldus-bolt of inspiration? Something tells me there's more to this than meets the eye."

Rockett gulped and exchanged a glance with Jessie. If Darnetta noticed, she didn't comment.

In the hallway, heading to her next class, she spied Ruben a few steps ahead. Impulsively, Rockett caught up and playfully tapped his arm. "Hey, Ruben — decided which fund-raiser you're gonna vote for?"

"Hey yourself, new girl." He grinned, slowing down a little. "No contest-o. I'm for Arrow's in-line skate-a-thon. I'm with the whole no-compete vibe and I think we can get local businesses to sponsor it. That takes the whole burden off the parents — the point, right?"

"I guess," Rockett agreed. Ruben's reasoning *was* on the mark.

Ruben stopped and motioned toward the classroom door they'd just reached. "Here's where I get off, language arts. How 'bout you? Where's your vote going?"

Rockett shook her head. "Not sure yet."

By the end of the day Rockett still hadn't written down her vote for the fund-raiser. After her last class, she wandered over to the Birdcage area — the school's bench-lined, domed entryway — and sat with the piece of paper on her lap, chewing the end of her pencil. When the bell rang for end-of-the-day homeroom, Rockett's ballot was still blank.

I better decide what to vote for — now! If I go with Arrow's idea, Ruben and I would totally have something in common. He was right, too: It is a cool suggestion. But the CSGs' student-teacher soccer game? How fun would that be? I should throw my support behind it — and them. But there's the calendar. Jessie thought of it first, after all. I probably could photograph and design it. That would be amazing! But isn't that kind of a selfish reason for voting for it?

Confession Session

Even though Nicole made like the calendar was her idea, I don't mind. I just want it to win, because that way, Rockett and Darnetta have a reason to work together. Which could make them better friends.

This idea stinks! Yeah, yeah, now Nicole and them are all over the calendar thing, but what if a guy — say, me — wanted to spend extra dough on the trip to get a gift for a certain someone? Now I can't? What crawled into the bizarre Baldus-brain that made him come up with this bogus idea, anyway? I'm gonna do some Diamond-class snooping.

CHAPTER FIVE

"And the winning idea for the class trip fund-raising project is . . . drumroll, please!" It's a good thing Mr. Baldus didn't have a microphone or any percussion instrument — amplification would have been redundant. His voice boomed as he theatrically waved an envelope in the air, as if he were announcing the Academy Awards.

"The Cool Kids of Whistling Pines Calendar!"

The class erupted spontaneously, cheering, sneering, and booing, all at the same time. Rockett, trying to contain her glee, observed the breakdown: Nakili, Miko, and Dana were chagrined; Ruben and Arrow, bummed. Arnold snorted his disappointment; Sharla, Wolf, and Mavis didn't react at all. Nicole and The Ones practically did a victory dance. Until, that is, Mr. Baldus reminded the class, "All potential posees should see our very own R-R-R-R-R-Rockett Movado: She is large and in charge!"

The Ones did an instant mood-180: They were severely unthrilled with that part of the plan. Still, they made the best of it.

Correction: the first of it.

The minute the bell rang, Nicole charged up to Rockett, armed with an elaborate sketch done in shaded pastels. "Here — don't thank me now. But we Ones have already made your job easier. We knew the calendar would win, so we worked it all out. See?"

Rockett looked. There were twelve colorful squares, labeled by month. Inside each one, a different person's school picture had been pasted in. Eleven were FONs: Friends of Nicole. The twelfth *was* Nicole.

"Um, thanks," Rockett murmured, scanning the design. "But you know what? I think I'll see who else wants to pose before going with this." With a confident tilt of her head, she handed the drawing back to Nicole and started to walk away.

Right. Like Nicole would let that happen. "You're not getting it." She inserted herself directly in Rockett's path. "It's called the *Cool* Kids of WP Calendar — not a Random Dorks of WP Calendar. And lucky for you there even *are* a dozen of us. Like I said, your job is handled — you're a mere figurehead. All that's left is taking the pictures. And I happen to have a window of opportunity this weekend for my close-up."

If Rockett hadn't been in such a kickin' mood, she would have balked at Nicole's nerve. But instead of blowing up, Rockett blew her off. "Let's revisit this tomorrow. I've got a lot to organize — and right now, if I don't hurry, I'll be late to art."

Although Nicole reluctantly complied, Rockett was late anyway. She could barely get from one end of the hallway to another without being stopped.

It suddenly seemed like half her grade — way more

than twelve kids, people who didn't even vote for it —
now wanted to be on the calendar. People like Ginger
Baskin and Viva Cortez, whom Rockett barely even
knew, stopped her to "apply." Each had a specific month
he or she wanted to be on.

"I'm posing for the July page, with my puppy,"
Stephanie announced regally. "It'll be so ca-*yute*! Can't
you just see it, Rockett?"

The lobbying continued through the day, in all of
Rockett's classes. Right at the start of social studies,
Cleve sauntered over, perched on the corner of her desk,
and casually instructed, "Put me down for January. I'm
gonna kick off the year, posing in my soccer uniform."
For effect, he kicked a pretend ball in the air.

"I want my picture to look exotic, like I'm from a far-
off land," Whitney wrote in the flourishy script in the
note she passed Rockett in science class. "Isn't that an
excellent idea? But what month? I'm thinking August."

The weird thing? Rockett realized she wasn't even
bummed by the bombardment of requests. She was kind
of . . . stoked.

I'm the go-to girl. Now it's, like, in the hallway? Every-
one's around me like a campfire — not like when I'm on the
outside of the circle, stressing if I should join in. And in class?
I'm the one they're passing notes to, instead of the in-between
girl. So this is what being popular feels like. Not too shabby!

Even when Arnold came up to Rockett in the middle
of computer lab, she didn't cringe, but paid rapt attention when he decided, "My idea was defeated, but I ac-

cept reversal of fortune. Instead, I will pose for the calendar."

Rockett's eyebrows shot up. "You will?"

Clearly, Arnold had thought this all out.

"I will, m'lady — in authentic shining armor."

It was only when he began to describe what he'd
wear — full Knights of the Round Table regalia — that
Rockett began to get a funny churning in her stomach.
She recognized the sensation: fear.

And it dawned on her . . .

. . . maybe this popularity thing had a downside.

. . . maybe she better have a plan — and quickly!

. . . maybe she needed Jessie's help.

She tried to find her bud *before* lunch — purposely so
they could talk without Darnetta being around. But
Jessie wasn't by her locker. She wasn't in the girls' room,
or the Birdcage, the track field, computer lab, or anywhere else Rockett could think of.

Reluctantly, Rockett headed into the lunchroom. *Too
late, I missed her. She's probably already sitting at our table.
With Darnetta. Maybe even with Mavis.*

But a quick scan of the cafeteria revealed — nuh-*uh*.
Darnetta and Mavis were there by themselves.

It was only when Rockett did a U-ie back into the
corridor to look around again that she finally found her.
Jessie was standing by an open locker — not her own.
She was talking to someone whose face was behind the
open locker door.

Psyched, Rockett called out, "Jessie! There you are! I

am so glad I found you before lunch. I've been looking all over for you."

Just as Jessie whirled around, the person behind the locker closed it.

Max.

Jessie's been with . . . him? All this time?

Jessie blushed tomato-red. "Oh, hi, Rockett. I didn't know you were looking for me."

Rockett stopped in her tracks and stammered, "Um, I sorta need your help. But we can do this . . . later."

Max jumped in. "Nah, go for it. I gotta find Cleve anyway. Later." With that, he bolted.

"Sorry, Jess," Rockett apologized when he was out of earshot. "Do I get the bad-timing award or what?"

Jessie, still blushing furiously, assured her, "Not even. I just, you know, ran into him and we started talking."

Rockett arched her eyebrows. *Jessie is so crushing on him! And it looks like he's feeling the same way. This is so sweet!*

"We were talking about, you know, the social studies homework. And stuff . . ." Jessie trailed off. "Anyway, what do you need me for?"

"The calendar."

Jessie brightened. "Isn't it awesome that it won? Did you vote for it?"

"I did," Rockett admitted, "even though I might have done it for selfish reasons."

"Because you're in charge and you get to design and photograph it?"

45

"Let me tell you, Jess, there's a definite downside to all this responsibility. It's out of control — everyone's asking to be in it. I need to come up with a plan and I need you. You're so good at this, and besides, you're the only one who knows the whole truth of why we're doing this. So Sharla can go on the trip."

Was it Rockett's imagination, or did Jessie just swallow really hard right then? She gazed up at Rockett through her fringe of bangs and answered quietly, "I'll do . . . what I can. Naturally."

"Thanks, Jess, I knew I could count on you."

The two friends strolled toward the cafeteria as Rockett explained her dilemma, and The Ones' idea: "Can you imagine, a 'We're all that and nobody else exists calendar'?"

Jessie laughed. "What would you expect from them?"

"If there's one thing I'm gonna do, it's make sure everyone has a fair shot at posing," Rockett declared. "Now if I could just figure out how."

Jessie stopped in her tracks and put her finger to her lips. Rockett could practically see the wheels in her head spinning. "How 'bout this? What if it's like, a Horoscope Calendar? Kids could pose on their birthday months. That would give us a fair sampling of all the different kinds of kids that make up our class."

Rockett lit up. "That rocks, Jessie! You always have the most creative solutions!"

Jessie grinned, flattered. "Yeah, I guess I do. Sometimes, anyway."

Rockett amended, "Even if it doesn't solve the problem of everyone wanting to be part of it. There *have* to be kids with the same signs and birthday months."

"Well," Jessie conceded, pushing open the cafeteria doors, "you'll have to pick and choose the best cross section. Just be as fair as you can — that'll be the tough part."

Understatement-alert. When Rockett spread the word that calendar-posing was going to be based on birthdays and would include horoscopes, the "choose me" request blitz intensified.

For as soon as kids found out who they were "up against," they lobbied her 24/7: in school, before and after school, at home, by e-mail, by note, by phone.

In class, she received dozens of passed notes. Every time she went to her locker, she found another note inside. *I am Miss July!* Stephanie had written, sounding suspiciously like some dippy beauty pageant contestant.

"Make me March," Darnetta had mentioned — a little too casually — at lunch.

Cleve, using magnetic poetry on her locker door, went with flattery. *I always thought you were cool, Rockett. By the way, I am all over April.*

Max resorted to bribery. On a card attached to a one-time-use camera, he'd printed, *Forget that whiny Weiss. Mr. October, I'm your man. Choose me, you know you can.*

Even Jessie was dropping hints that she'd be a much better bet for February than Arnold. And, BTW: Wouldn't Max look cute in October?

You have to choose me for October, Whitney had scrawled, *because we are friends — always remember that.*

Whitney attempted to "prove" that later in the day. During a volleyball match in PE when it was Rockett's serve, Whitney tossed her the ball — along with a stage-whispered invitation. "A bunch of us are going to that new FunScape amusement park on Saturday. Why don't you come?"

Stephanie leaned over to second the invite, adding, "We're going for pizza afterward."

Rockett grasped the volleyball a little longer than she should have. *Should I? It could be cool. I mean, when they're not acting all snobby, they can really be fun. But reality check: I'm sure they only invited me because they want to be on the calendar. I should say no — on principle. But then, they all might turn against me, even Whitney, who I really like.*

And sometimes I like Stephanie. I hardly know Chaz, but Max and Cleve are kinda fun. If I went, maybe Max would say something about his crush on Jessie. Wouldn't that be interesting! If the only reason to say, "No way" is because of Nicole, that's lame. And so what if they're only inviting me because of the calendar thing? Once they get to know me — especially away from school — they'll find I'm a totally cool person. That would be worth going for. Probably.

Whomp! Because Rockett got distracted, Dana snuck up and whipped the ball away from her, snarling, "Either serve or get off the court, Movado! Their side is winning, in case you hadn't noticed!"

48

CHAPTER SIX

If time had stopped in the middle of the day on Saturday, Rockett might have tagged it as one of her best days ever at Whistling Pines. Even if they *had* invited her for selfish reasons, she was having a blast with The Ones.

There was a reason everyone envied them — and it went beyond their elitist attitude. The Ones totally knew how to blow out and have the most kickin' fun. They could even be extra nice, especially Whitney, Stephanie, Cleve, Chaz, and Max. That day, even Nicole was on her best behavior.

"Your hair looks cute like that," she'd mentioned as she opened the car door for Rockett. Nicole's father was driving this way-expensive sport utility wagon, and everyone was already packed inside.

"Okay, Reginald, this is all of us," Nicole said. "We can head straight to FunScape."

Reginald? I thought this is her dad — it can't be a chauffeur, can it?

As if Whitney could read Rockett's mind, she whispered, "Nic always calls her parents by their first names. It's sort of a family tradition."

Rockett, who slid into the backseat next to Whitney, arched her eyebrows as if to say, *How weird*.

In response, Whitney shrugged.

But it was Reginald's remark to his daughter as he dropped the gang off at the amusement park that Rockett found weirdest of all.

"Remember, Nicole, I'm granting you this little diversion only because of that A+ you brought home in language arts. Next Saturday, you'll have to make up that extra computer class."

"Got it, Reginald," Nic had said through gritted teeth.

Her dad added, "What do I always say? To be the best, you've got to stay ahead of the competition. Now — I expect you to be home by dinner. You've got that extra-credit assignment to work on."

Wow! Her dad's really strict. I never imagined that!

What Rockett had imagined, and what turned out to be totally true, was that on the loose at FunScape, The Ones' good-time vibes really ramped up. The place was a combination carnival, arcade, and amusement park. Rockett went on a killer log flume ride, sitting next to Whitney, who squealed at every dip and grabbed Rockett's arm when they got splashed.

She beat Nicole at skee ball — and the haughty One was actually nice about it. "Sports are so not my thing," Nicole had conceded, "but you've really got a way of keeping your eye on the ball, Rockett. You should probably try out for soccer."

And when Chaz won a stuffed owl, he gave it to her.

"I noticed that you sometimes wear an owl pendant, so I figured maybe you'd be into this."

He was right. Owls were among Rockett's favorite birds: She had an entire collection. She hadn't really figured him for being that observant — he'd barely said two words to her until very recently. *Well, maybe I figured wrong about a lot of Ones-related things.*

Or not.

Things didn't go downhill until much later in the day. This time it was Max's dad — in a luxury vehicle even more elaborate than Nicole's — who picked up the posse. He dropped them off at Let's Get Some 'Za, the trendy new pizza place The Ones had declared "in."

Whitney and Max began to one-up each other about their "friendly" competition to pose for the school calendar's October page. Whitney went flirty, resting her head on Max's shoulder. "I would look so much better on the calendar than you would — come on, just give up trying, okay?"

And Max, pushing Whitney's frizzy locks out of his eyes, retorted, "But with your hair taking up so much space, there wouldn't be room for the days of the month!"

To which Whitney, jerking her head up, shot back, "My hair doesn't take up nearly as much room as your ego."

Still, it wasn't as if the two ruined the afternoon by waging a full-scale battle or anything.

They left that to Nicole and Chaz.

With Rockett smack in the middle of the booth, between the once-friendly opponents.

51

To Rockett's left was Chaz.

To her right, Nicole.

Both celebrated birthdays in August. And, like Whitney and Max, both very much wanted to represent that page.

Chaz, no doubt picking up where Whitney and Max left off, made a casual comment about what he was planning to wear for his photo session. "I think I photograph best in blue. What's your take on that, Rockett?"

Before she could respond, Nicole sprang into action. She grasped Rockett's shoulder, forcing a face-to-face. Her insolent green eyes flashing, she huffed, "Excuse me? Why would you even consider him for one second? I'm actually going to be a model one day. My picture will be worth money!"

For emphasis she scarfed a large bite of pizza.

Chaz immediately put his hand on Rockett's other shoulder. He countered with diplomacy, "All the more reason to choose me — it's just a simple student calendar, after all, nothing professional. Nicole's too glam. I'm more representative of the real deal at Whistling Pines."

He chomped off a bigger piece of his slice.

Nicole went deeper into the offensive zone. Again, she forced Rockett to turn her way. "If for some bizarre reason you don't choose me? Your name will be synonymous with anonymous! I will personally see to it that you are snubbed by everyone who matters here."

She slurped her drink noisily.

Chaz scoffed. "Come on, Rockett. You can't let her intimidate you. Not to toot my own horn or anything, but she's not the only One in the school. Stick with me, and your status here will not suffer one bit. I personally guarantee it."

He slurped his drink — louder.

Nicole resorted to bottom-line tactics. "If I'm in the calendar, my daddy will pledge to buy one hundred of them! Can you even count how much we'll raise then? But if I'm not in it . . . ? You do the math!"

She held her crust up menacingly — ready to fling it at Chaz.

Chaz's eyes clouded. "Bribery? She's going with that? Desperation. But if we're going down that path, let me assure you that the entire Franklin clan will make it worth the school's while if I'm in August."

On that last word, Nicole did pitch a piece of pizza crust at him, nailing his shoulder. Grimacing, Chaz retaliated with some gooey cheese picked off the top of his slice. He aimed straight at Nicole's hair: His aim was true.

She went ballistic, screaming and tossing bits from her salad, the sugar on the table, anything within reach. "Take that!"

Whitney and Max got into it. In a matter of seconds, food was flying everywhere!

Stephanie and Cleve tried to stop the insanity, but they weren't fast or effective enough: The manager stomped over and demanded they leave.

It didn't matter. Rockett was no longer hungry. She had a crushing headache.

And one question: *I came along with them . . . exactly why? What was I thinking?*

The following Monday afternoon, Rockett was lost in thought, walking toward her locker. She didn't even notice the girl headed her way — until a lilting voice interrupted her reverie. "Hey, stress puppy, wassup?"

Instantly, Rockett broke into a grin. "Hey yourself, Nakili! Is it that obvious?"

She nodded. "Girl, you are definitely somewhere else."

"I'm just sorta deeply distracted."

"Let me guess. The 'I'm large and in charge of the calendar thing,' huh?"

"It's . . . uh . . . kind of hard to do it fairly, and not make enemies of certain people," Rockett explained. "Not to mention, get in the middle of their battles."

Nakili shrugged. "So why not ask for help deciding?"

Rockett was about to blurt that she would ask Jessie — like always — but Jessie, lobbying on behalf of herself *and* her crush, Max, was part of the problem. It took a second before she got that Nakili was offering . . . herself.

"Would you?" Rockett asked gratefully.

"Dilemma-busters diva service — at your disposal. Come to my house after school and break it down for me. If *I* can't come up with a fair solution, maybe there isn't one."

Relief coursed through Rockett. "That's so cool,

Nakili. . . ." She trailed off before adding, "Will, uh, the others be there, too?"

Nakili shook her head. "Miko's gotta get with her sister to shop for their mom's birthday present, and Dana's taking her dog to the vet."

Rockett had been over to Nakili's before, but she'd never had much chance to really look around. This time, she did. All over Nakili's bedroom walls were photos of the CSGs that ranged from kindergarten to junior high, prominently featuring the threesome: at the beach, horseback riding, their faces painted at a carnival, trick-or-treating.

"You guys really do go way back, huh?" Rockett remarked.

"Pull up a floor," Nakili said before responding, and plopped down on her lavender carpet. "Yeah, we got that history thing going. But you know, Rockett, sometimes history isn't all that. Sometimes, you gotta look ahead."

Before Rockett could delve further, Nakili switched subjects. "So let's see if we can solve this baby."

Rockett took out her notebook. She'd started a whole section for the calendar, working up potential designs and making lists, matching people to their birthday months. "Let's start with the easy ones. Since each eighth-grade homeroom is doing a separate calendar, at least there are a few months in ours with no competition."

"Sounds like a plan," Nakili agreed. "Lay it on me."

Rockett read off the 'no problem' list. "March, Darnetta. April, Cleve; June, Ginger. Then, in September — well, there's Viva and Sharla, but I know Sharla wouldn't want it, so I think it's an easy choice. In November, there's just Miko."

Nakili noted, "And you can add December to that. There's me and Dana, but I'm giving it to her."

"You sure?"

"Absolutely. It means more to her than to me — so I say let her have it."

"That's . . . cool of you, Nakili."

"Anyway, that's nearly half the months right there — done! See why it's easier to do this with another person? Helps you see the real deal. Go on to the tough choices."

Rockett flipped a page in her notebook and took a deep breath. "Well, in January there's really only one person, but it's sort of a dilemma anyway. 'Cause I'm pretty sure he doesn't want to pose."

"Let me guess," Nakili said, snapping her fingers. "Wolf DuBois?"

"How'd you know?"

"'Cause I've been going to school with him since elementary. And you're right, he's tough to figure. He may act a certain way, but you can't take him at face value."

"Huh?" Now Rockett was really confused.

"I'm just sayin' the boy's got layers — he's complicated."

Rockett thought about it. "The only thing I really know about Wolf is that he's Native American, he keeps to himself — and of course, that Nicole has been kinda crushing on him."

Nakili laughed derisively. "A crush that will never be reciprocated! No way would he go for someone as superficial as Nicole."

"Interesting. So you think that even though Wolf hasn't said a word to me about wanting to pose, maybe he really does."

"Could be. Just tell him, 'Tag, you're it: January.' Now, who's down for February?"

"There's . . . uh . . . Arnold Zeitbaum, who — wait'll you hear this! — wants to pose as a medieval knight! And there's Jessie."

Nakili chuckled. "No contest. You gotta go with your best bud — Jessie, of course."

Rockett surprised herself with the intensity of her reaction. "She's not my best. I mean, she's my good friend . . . she's been a lot of help . . . the calendar was her idea."

"So how can you not include her?"

"I should," Rockett conceded. "But then Arnold's feelings will be hurt."

"Some people *are* gonna feel bad for a moment," Nakili reminded her gently. "But Arnold? He's such a zany brainy. He'll forget it soon enough."

Rockett resisted. "I'm not so sure, Nakili. Even though he acts weird — okay, really weird — he just gets dissed so much, it's gotta hurt. Wouldn't it be a cool thing to let him win . . . sorta . . . at least once?"

Nakili softened. "Your heart's in the right place, Rockett. And under normal circumstances, I'd say go for it. But in this one, he's up against Jessie. You said yourself how the whole thing was her idea, how she always helps you."

Rockett didn't commit — she couldn't. Not yet. "Let me think about it," she told Nakili before going on. "Okay, here's another tricky sitch. In May, there's Ruben and also Arrow."

"Who wants it?"

"That's the thing, I'm not sure either one does. They both voted for the in-line skating thing to win. I think they might still be wiggin'."

"They told you that?"

"No . . . but . . ."

"You don't know, then. Just pick one of them anyway — I say Ruben."

Rockett blanched. *Does she know I like him?* "Why?"

"Easy," Nakili replied. "I'm keeping an informal count, and it looks like you're gonna need guys to make it more even. Watch and see if I'm not right."

Rockett frowned. "Let's go on. August. That one's already gotten pretty nasty. It's Nicole. And Chaz. And they are seriously fighting about it."

Nakili slapped her thigh. "Two Ones divided against themselves — who knows? Maybe the whole clique will implode!"

"That's too much to hope for, and you know it." Rock-

58

ett giggled. Nakili had a way of totally lightening things up.

"Anyway, you gotta go with Chaz. You'll need boys, I'm tellin' ya'."

"But Nicole will . . ."

"Will what? Don't tell me you're afraid of her — come on!"

Rockett retorted, "Afraid of her? As if. I'm just trying to be fair. I'll come back to that one. Besides, here's the worst of it: In October, there's, like, three — Mavis, Max, and Whitney."

"Do they all want to be included?" Nakili asked.

"Two out of three — definitely. But I kinda think that Mavis might want to, she's just too shy to ask. Still, that shouldn't automatically eliminate her, right?"

Nakili sighed. "You always make things harder than they have to be. If Mavis isn't interested, for whatever reason, let it go. Then you just have to choose between Max and Whitney."

"And how am I going to do that? Whitney and I, well, we get along. Even though she can be such a snob sometimes . . ."

"You're friends." Nakili's tone was nonjudgmental.

"Pretty much, yeah."

"Well, that's one way to decide."

"But wait. I have a pretty strong feeling Jessie wants me to choose Max."

Nakili arched her eyebrows. "Rewind?"

Rockett paused, then let it spill. "I, well, I'm sure she wouldn't mind if I told you: Jessie kinda likes him. And I think the feeling's mutual."

Nakili's eyes widened. "Never would've guessed! So Jessie will be bent outta shape if you pick Whitney, huh?"

"She hasn't exactly said so. But she's been so great helping me with ideas and support and stuff. I just . . ."

"Owe her?"

Rockett scrunched her nose. "I wish you wouldn't put it that way."

"It is what it is, Rockett. But it's your choice — I can't help you with that one. But what's up with July? You skipped right over it. Isn't that your month?"

Rocket blushed. In a way, she kinda hoped Nakili wouldn't notice. She felt a little wimpy about her reasoning. "Busted. Stephanie Hollis has been campaigning for that from the get-go. So I guess I'll just let her have it."

"How selfless of you — especially since she's not your friend. Don't you want to be in your own calendar?"

"Sure I do, but how self-serving would that seem?"

"Forget that. Look at it this way. Stephanie Hollis is a One. She gets everything she wants anyway. And if the tables were turned, would she let you just have it? I don't think so, Rockett."

The afternoon at Nakili's had given Rockett a lot to think about. True, some choices were now practically made. But others were still tough. Rockett spent all night

60

tossing and turning. She had four major decisions to make.

Jessie or Arnold? Okay, on the Jessie side, maybe she's not my best friend, but she is a true friend. She always listens to my problems. And I know she can keep a secret — like the reason we're really doing this in the first place. I should just pick her.

But I feel so bad for Arnold! Just because he's not popular and acts weird sometimes — okay, most of the time — does that mean I should do what everyone else does, just ignore him? I'm not like everyone else. I'm an independent thinker.

Then there's Ruben and Arrow. If I pick Ruben, how obvious will it be that I'm crushing on him? And what if he turns me down? Will that mean he doesn't like me? Arrow would be the more neutral choice. But if I do that, Ruben might think I don't like him. I definitely don't want to send that message!

As for Whitney and Max, I should probably just toss a coin. I like Whitney, she's fun to hang with. But Max . . . every time I think of him, I can't help thinking of Jessie. Will she think I betrayed her if I choose Whitney? On the other hand, Jessie's pretty forgiving.

And here's the ickiest one of all. Nicole and Chaz. I don't like being threatened by Nicole — but Chaz suddenly acting like he's my NBF, what's that about? They're both phonies. I'm just going to go with . . . aaahh! Remind me how I got myself into this!!

CHAPTER SEVEN

Partly, it was Nakili's advice, and partly Jessie's, that led Rockett to her final choices. By the time she finally turned out the light and went to sleep, she had her list. Her plan was to get to homeroom early, talk to Mr. Baldus, and then let the class know who'd been chosen.

Only . . . Rockett didn't end up getting to homeroom early. She got to school way before the first bell, but a funny thing happened on the way to Baldus's class: She ran into someone. Someone who was usually tardy; never, as far as Rockett knew, early. Someone who'd obviously been waiting for her. And was definitely happy-challenged.

Caught off guard, Rockett stammered, "Hi, what are you . . ." but Sharla Rae Norvell, scowling and furious, didn't let her finish. She pointed down the hallway and commanded, "Girls' room, Movado — now!"

Rockett felt wobbly. *What does she want with me? She can't be mad — she doesn't know anything. But what's up with the scary tone? I'm not afraid of her. I should say, "Anything you have to say to me, you can say here." But what if she wants to share something personal — and she's just tense? That could be it. Or maybe she does want to pick a fight! Uh-oh, now I am scared!*

As she allowed Sharla to lead her to the girls' room, Rockett nervously chattered nonstop. "What's up with the secret meeting, Sharla? I didn't expect to see you here. I got here early because I'm going to announce the choices for the calendar. I know you're September, but . . ."

With a forced slam of the bathroom door, Sharla silenced her. "You've got some nerve, Movado!"

Folding her arms across her chest defensively, Rockett retreated — until she felt the small of her back against the sink. In, okay, a really lame attempt to lighten the moment, she heard herself quip, "I'm not getting this. Can I, uh, buy a vowel?"

Sharla was unamused. "Get off it. You can't even lie with a straight face. You know exactly what this is about."

"Um, actually, I don't . . ." Rockett trailed off. The look in Sharla's eyes — half acid glare, half hurt — forced her to amend. "That is, I'm not sure."

"Oh, really?" Sharla pointed a sharp finger at Rockett's nose. "Then let me educate you. You set up this whole elaborate 'let's raise money for the trip' thing for me — poor little Sharla, the charity case! How dare you?!"

Rockett was stunned. *She knows! How could she know?* She stammered, "It . . . I . . . how did you find out?"

Sharla leaned in closer to Rockett and growled, "Like you care. Who do you think you are, anyway, to get in my business like that? And besides, where did you even get the lamebrained idea that I couldn't afford to go?"

Should I tell her about finding her note — and reading it?

She might really blow up at me then! But I'm not great at lying. What would I say, anyway?

Hyper, Rockett furtively glanced at the bathroom door, willing someone to come in and rescue her. Even Nicole would have been a welcome sight!

But Sharla was staring at her menacingly. "I repeat, RoMo — where did you come up with this idea?"

Rockett gulped. She felt sick. She whispered, "It's all because of this letter someone left on the floor of the girls' room. It was about not wanting to go on the class trip because of not having enough money."

Sharla stiffened and quickly turned away. Quietly, she said, "Why did you assume it was mine?"

Rockett exhaled. "Something about the way it was written. And that same day, you were . . . I mean, I saw you . . . crying. In the bathroom. So I kind of put two and two together. . . ."

Sharla whirled around, filled again with rage. "And came up with six! You are certifiable, Movado."

Half-whispering, Rockett asked, "The letter wasn't yours? You weren't crying?"

All at once, the air seemed to go out of Sharla. She brushed past Rockett and gripped the side of the sink. She looked like she was going to be sick.

"Are you okay?" Rockett asked tentatively, taking a step toward her.

"Okay? Of course not! You made sure of that." She paused. "Get this straight. I owe you nothing, not even an explanation. But yeah, okay, the letter was mine, so what? That's the only thing you got right."

"The only thing?" Rockett repeated. "So you mean . . . you're not . . . you have enough money? And you weren't crying?"

"Crying? Yeah, right. Like I'd break down for a pathetic sob-fest in this place! Never! And maybe I don't look it to you — but I have all the money I need if I even wanted to go. Which I don't. Oh, and here's that vowel you asked for: O. It goes between M, Y, and B. I'll solve the puzzle for you: MYOB!"

Rockett's heart thudded. "I'm sorry, Sharla, I only wanted to help."

"Help? All you did was make it worse for me. Now the whole school thinks I'm such a loser I can't even scrape together chump change to buy a stupid souvenir on the trip! How do you think that makes me feel?"

Rockett blurted, "I thought you didn't care what anyone thinks of you."

"I don't — not in this place! But when you invade other people's privacy — like reading their letters — bad things happen. Like this!" She started to walk out the door, but Rockett stopped her.

"Sharla, wait. If it wasn't the money, then why did you write that line about 'no dough'? And . . . uh . . . who's Nigel?"

Sharla shook her head and let out a long sigh. "Nigel's my pen pal. He lives in England. We tell each other stuff — stuff that's no one else's business. So I told him I don't want to go on the trip, which happens to be true."

"But why say it's about the money ... if it isn't?" Rockett asked softly.

"Because he doesn't have a lot of money, so he could relate. Besides, he doesn't know everything about me, so why tell him the real reason?"

"Which is ... ?"

Her face twisted into a grimace. "One guess."

"Because you don't have any ... um ... you know, like ..."

"Friends? No one likes me, right? So I'd probably get stuck sitting next to one of the teachers, and rooming with, I don't know, some other loser. Come on, you've gone this far, spit it out. That's what you were going to say, wasn't it?"

Rockett gulped. She mumbled, "I know what it's like. ..."

But the expression on Sharla's face stopped her. "*You* know what it's like? Yeah, right."

Without thinking, Rockett blurted, "The class trip is going to be awesome! It isn't about having friends. It's about a big, exciting city and an ultra-cool art museum — there's a whole world beyond Whistling Pines. And I don't know you that well, but I'm guessing that deep down you really would like to go. Someone who writes poetry, you've gotta want to see more. Only maybe you're afraid of ..."

"Nothing! I'm not afraid of anything, Rockett. Except meddling do-gooders like you."

At that second, Rockett knew it was all right. For Sharla's voice had finally softened. And that gave her the courage to say, "I never meant for anyone to find out that the fund-raiser was on someone's behalf — and how stupid do I feel now, knowing how wrong I was all along? And . . ." She paused. "I know I don't have the right to ask . . . but, well, how did you find out?"

Wordlessly, Sharla dug into her back pocket and took out a note. She handed it to Rockett.

The words on it were neat — and to the point.

Thanks a lot, Norvell. If it wasn't for you being such a loser, we wouldn't have to raise money for the trip. We wouldn't be doing this dumb calendar — where they stole my idea and put a nerd in charge. Like I said, thanks for nothing.

Rockett's jaw dropped. *Nicole strikes again.*

Sharla's eyes had started to tear.

And Rockett had never felt lower. Trembling, she offered, "My mega-bad, Sharla. I am so incredibly sorry."

Sharla sniffled and wiped her eyes with her shirtsleeve. "Right. Thanks, Rockett. Thanks for nothing."

As she bolted out the door, Rockett desperately yelled after her. "Please reconsider. Go on the trip, Sharla, it'll be . . ."

She wanted to say *fun*. But at that second, she wasn't even sure she believed that.

How did this happen? How'd I make such a mess of this? That's what I get for reading someone else's private letter — and then jumping to a duh-headed conclusion. All I did was make enemies. But . . . how did Nicole, of all people, find out? There's only one other person who knew. Someone I totally trusted.

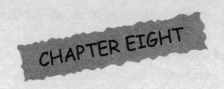

CHAPTER EIGHT

Rockett was determined to collar Jessie — but time was so not on her side. A few minutes after her face-off with Sharla, she stood in front of her homeroom — knowing that what she was about to announce would have a major effect on her classmates. Some people would be totally psyched, but she'd probably make some enemies, too. And all for what? Nothing, obviously.

Still, there was no turning back now. At least Sharla had skipped homeroom. *She* wouldn't have to face anyone.

Rockett gripped the side of Mr. Baldus's desk so hard her knuckles turned white. She wished the catch in her voice wasn't so obvious. "I want to start by saying that making these choices was really tough. And . . . um, I really tried to be as fair as possible, and have the calendar be representative of . . . well . . . a cross section of us."

"Yo, Rockett, just spill it," Max called out, brimming with confidence.

As twenty-five pairs of eyes stared at her, she steeled herself, took a deep breath, and delivered.

"January: Wolf DuBois." Rockett looked at him for a reaction.

But Wolf only twisted his fingers around the leather

cord of the Arctic wolf canine tooth he always wore around his neck, and said nothing.

"February: Jessie Marbella."

Darnetta whooped and Jessie blushed — obviously psyched. Rockett was afraid to look Arnold's way, but when she did she found that Arnold's head was in his hands, his eyes focused on his desk. Rockett felt crummy.

Announcing Darnetta for March, and Cleve for April — two people she knew she'd just made happy — didn't make her feel any better. Nor did saying Ruben's name for May. Arrow seemed cool with it and Ruben, for all his nonchalance, looked pretty stoked.

Giving June to Ginger had been an easy decision. As was telling Stephanie she could pose for July. Above Nakili's objections, Rockett had decided that she'd feel too selfish choosing herself.

"August . . ." Rockett's heart started to thump so loudly, she was sure the whole class could hear it. "Chaz Franklin."

Nicole's eyes flared. Choked with rage, she blasted Rockett. "Bad choice!" Then she stormed out of the room.

Rockett looked at Mr. Baldus expectantly. Would he go after her? Give her detention? He just shook his head, as if to say, *Forget it*.

What he did say was, "You're doing great, continue."

She talked quickly — as if that would stem the tide of more outbursts. "Okay. Um, for September, we'll have Viva Cortez. And for October . . . uh . . ." Rockett made the mistake of eyeballing Whitney. Because she could see

72

the hurt in her eyes as she announced, "Max Diamond." Everyone could hear Max's self-congratulatory "Oh, yeah, way to go."

November had gone to Miko, December to Dana.

And it was over.

Shakily, Rockett returned to her seat. She barely heard Mr. Baldus thanking her for a tough job well done, and giving instructions to the class about collecting pledges since the actual calendars wouldn't be ready for a while. She only heard him finish by saying, "We'll schedule photo sessions as soon as we get back from our trip — which, I don't have to remind you, is next week!"

Jessie was by Rockett's side the minute the bell rang. "Amazing choices, Rockett. You did the best job. We've got real diversity in the calendar now. You should be really proud of yourself."

Clearly, Jessie wasn't prepared for Rockett's response. "Proud of myself? Maybe. And maybe someone else should be really ashamed of herself."

Jessie blanched, confused. "What . . . are you talking about, Rockett?"

Rocket was closer to tears than she wanted to be. "Look, Jessie, I have to go to first-period class now. But we need to talk. Meet me in the girls' room during lunch."

Rockett couldn't help herself. She tossed in what she knew was over the top. "Come alone — if you think you can manage that."

Jessie's eyes widened and her voice croaked. "Why are you being like this? This isn't like you at all."

"We'll talk about who's not being like herself later." Rockett brushed past Jessie, leaving them both feeling lousy.

The rest of the morning didn't lighten Rockett's mood. Although several kids, like Ginger, Viva, and Stephanie, went out of their way to thank her, and others she hadn't chosen gave her props for being fair, Sharla avoided her. Whitney shot her hurt expressions. Even Arnold snubbed her by walking past without making eye contact. Rockett stayed as far as she could from Nicole.

The morning seemed to stretch interminably. When the fifth-period bell rang, signaling lunch, Rockett raced to the girls' room. She was pretty sure she'd beat Jessie there: but not even.

Jessie was majorly upset. "What's going on, Rockett? You're really making me nervous."

The look on Jessie's freckled face was so open and trusting, it lessened some of Rockett's anger. But she had to know: Had Jessie spilled the secret?

"Sharla found out. Someone told her that this whole fund-raising thing was for her. Now she thinks the whole school knows and she blames me. How could that have happened, Jessie? You're the only one I told."

Jessie's hand flew to her mouth. She gasped. "I . . . didn't tell her. Promise."

Rockett peered at Jessie intently. Because suddenly, she got it. "You told someone else, though, right? That's how it spread and got back to her."

Jessie didn't really have to answer. Rockett knew she'd told Max. Who'd told Nicole. Who couldn't wait to tell Sharla and make her feel bad. For the bonus round, she got to make Rockett look like a fool.

Now Jessie was beside herself — totally torn. "I didn't mean for this to happen. You have to believe me. Max, well, it's just that he was complaining about the calendar thing because he wanted to take more money. He wanted to buy me a present, a souvenir on the trip. Isn't that sweet? And he thought he wouldn't be able to. I only told him the truth so he'd be for the fund-raiser, not against it."

Rockett's face was impassive.

Jessie blurted, "I made him promise not to tell anyone."

"Obviously, his promises don't count for much, Jessie." Rockett knew that was harsh. But not as bad as the next thing she let fly. "And neither do yours. I trusted you."

Jessie swallowed hard. She crossed her arms in front of her chest. "I'm sorry you feel that way, Rockett. I never . . . told anything you didn't want me to before this. And . . ." she blurted, "how do you think it makes *me* feel to always have to keep your secrets — and not be able to tell anyone? You think that's always so easy?" With that, Jessie walked out of the girls' room.

Shaken, Rockett didn't know what to do. She heard footsteps — without thinking, she slipped into a stall. The next sound she heard was Nicole, sniffing. "At least there's a silver lining."

"What's that?" Whitney, apparently, was with her.

75

"At least we don't have to suck up to Rockett anymore. That day we let her come with us to the amusement park like some kind of dork outreach program. Was that not the pits? It will so not be replayed."

Whitney giggled — nervously.

Nicole added, "Of course that's not nearly enough for her punishment."

The hairs on the back of Rockett's neck stood up.

Carefully, Whitney asked, "What do you mean? What are you planning?"

"Not planning. Already done. When I first found out that Rockett arranged this fund-raiser for Sharla, I only told those on a need-to-know basis. That is, you, Steph, Cleve, and Chaz. Today I made sure the whole school knows. Result? Sharla feels even worse — like I care! — and Rockett gets a taste of her own medicine. She knows what it's like to feel betrayed."

"Betrayed?" For a sec, Whitney seemed confused.

"She betrayed both of us, Whitney. I mean, Max is a friend and all — but picking him instead of you? And then making it worse by picking Chaz instead of me? Has that girl got a plate in her head or what?"

Rockett trudged through the rest of her day, feeling majorly miserable. The cloud didn't lift until she opened her locker at the very end of the day. There, on the floor — slipped through the vents, obviously — someone had dropped a folded-up note.

Great. This is probably some kind of poison pen letter

from another member of America's Most Disgruntled. I probably shouldn't even open it. But I can't tell whose handwriting this is — it could be from Jessie, I guess, saying what she couldn't say in person?

The note wasn't from Jessie. Rockett didn't know who it was from. Only that it clearly came from the bottom of someone's heart.

Dear Rockett,
    I know you probably feel bad now. That's why I'm writing this. To make you feel better. Thanks to Nicole, the whole school now knows you tried to do this for Sharla and that you made a humongo mistake — Sharla's going around telling everyone she can so afford it. She didn't need your help and next time, you better mind your own business!
    But what no one knows is that someone else did need your help, Rockett. That someone is me. For my own secret reasons, I really need to go on this trip. But I don't have a spare dollar even. And everyone would have found out when I couldn't even buy a soda, or any souvenirs. Now I can go, and no one will ever know, or be able to tease me. So thank you, Rockett. I can't tell you who I am. But just thank you.

Rockett reread the note, dozens of times. She had no clue who wrote it.

Confession Session

Tell me this didn't happen. I should have known Max can't keep a secret. Not from his real friends — The Ones. What was I thinking? I know I should tell Rockett how sorry I am. But I meant what I said. Sometimes it really isn't fun being her friend. Anyway, I guess she's right to be mad at me. I need to talk to 'Netta — she'll know what to do.

That Rockett! She really turned against me — I mean, to pick Max over me! She doesn't even like him. Until she learns a thing or two about friendship and loyalty, we'll never really be close. Days like this make me see who my real friends are, and why I stick with Nic.

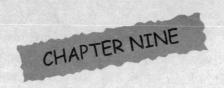

CHAPTER NINE

"Hey, Rockett, who are you sitting next to on the bus to Chicago?"

Miko's question, asked as the girls were gathering their books after art class, was totally casual. She couldn't know she'd hit on one of two kinda huge issues: who Rockett would sit with, and who'd she room with in Chicago. At least the roomie thing could wait a while.

"I'm not exactly sure yet," Rockett answered warily.

The past few days had gone by at warp speed. The calendar fund-raiser was finally over and in spite of the turmoil, it turned out to be a huge success. So many parents and teachers had pledged to buy copies that each eighth grader was going to get a fair amount of spending money on the trip. And as Rockett now understood, that had made a certain someone — not Sharla, but some secret person — majorly grateful.

So Rockett felt vindicated. Sort of. But now that the whole thing was over, Rockett was no longer the "go-to" girl, she was just . . . herself again. Correction: herself with enemies she didn't have before — put Whitney in that category! And worse, without the one person who came closest, so far, to being her best friend, Jessie.

Rockett knew that Jessie felt guilty. And that Darnetta was the person who made Jessie feel better.

All of which left her . . . well, out of the loop again.

And two days before the class trip — was there a worse time to feel friend-challenged? Rockett didn't think so! She wanted someone cool to sit with on the bus, and to room with at the hotel in Chicago. In spite of what she'd said to Sharla about the trip not just being about friends. . . . Without them, even an amazing class trip wouldn't be much fun.

Rockett regarded Miko as they headed to their second-period classes. Although she was pretty sure she knew the answer, she ventured, "Who are you sitting with?"

"Dana. We're choosing who gets the window. Probably she'll get it on the way there, me on the way back."

Hopefully, Rockett inquired, "What about Nakili?"

Miko shrugged. "I'm not sure who she was going to ask."

Maybe she hasn't asked anyone yet — better get moving! Nakili would probably be my first choice anyway, after Jessie.

As soon as she sat down in math class, Rockett scribbled a note and passed it to Nakili.

Her answer came back almost instantly. "I asked Sharla. Everybody knows what's been going down with her, and it just felt like someone should do something, try to make her feel part of it. You started it, Rockett. Now I'm all over it."

Rockett whirled around and threw Nakili a surprised look. She mouthed, "Sharla's going?"

Nakili's nod was accompanied by a megawatt smile.

And Rockett couldn't help a half-smile back. *Maybe some good will come out of this after all!* That thought helped brighten her morning. She even felt optimistic about finding someone to sit with.

During third-period social studies, the class was asked to list the major turning points of the Civil War. After Rockett had jotted down Gettysburg and Sherman's march through Atlanta, she turned to the next page in her notebook and made another list: *Who can I sit with?* By the end of the period, after writing down names and then erasing most of them, she was left with four potential people.

She decided to ask the first person on her list.

Jessie.

What have I got to lose? Maybe this will be a chance to get our friendship back on track. One of my best qualities: I don't stay mad. And okay, there's a good chance Jessie has already made plans with Darnetta. But if she wants to really make it up to me . . . well, plans can change.

Optimistically, Rockett headed to fourth-period science, which Jessie also had. This time she didn't send a note, but collared her freckled friend outside the classroom door just before the bell rang, and breezily suggested, "So, Jess, what do you say we sit together on the bus ride to Chicago?"

Jessie was anything but breezy. She stammered, "I . . . wow, Rockett, that's so awesome to ask me. I never thought you would. Does this mean . . . you're not mad at me anymore about telling Max?"

Rockett tilted her head. "I don't hold a grudge. But I would like to talk to you . . . about everything. And sitting together on the bus would give us that chance."

Jessie took a deep breath.

And frowned. "I have to be honest, I already said I'd sit with 'Netta."

Rockett feigned nonchalance as she waited for Jessie to add, "But I could change my plans."

That offer never came.

Because Rockett didn't want to seem desperate or anything, she quickly filled the awkward silence. "That's cool, Jessie. And as for the Max thing, I guess we can talk about it another time." She wasn't letting Jessie off the hook that easily!

In retrospect, Rockett realized she probably should have taken Jessie's turn-down as a sign: She might not fare any better with the next person on her list. But just before lunch, she bravely walked straight up to Whitney.

Ready, aim, misfire.

Whitney, who'd appeared approachable, morphed into full drama mode. Mouth agape, she blasted, "You actually have the nerve to ask me to sit with you? As if *that's* going to make your choosing Max over me, like, okay? You have a lot to learn about friendship, Rockett." And then, with a deliberate click of her platforms, she stalked away.

Whitney's diss dampened Rockett's resolve. It took her until eighth-period PE to feel ready to try again. Luckily both people left on her list were in that class. One was on her right, doing warm-up stomach crunches: Arrow.

She was a possibility for two reasons. They weren't really friends, but they'd talked a few times, and kinda liked each other. Also, Arrow had two best buds — Viva and Ginger — one of them could potentially be seatmate-challenged.

There was also the girl on Rockett's left, Mavis. It was a good bet *she* didn't have anyone to sit with. And to be totally honest, Rockett knew Mavis a lot better than she knew Arrow. It made more sense to ask her. But on crunch number 25, Rockett let out a huge sigh. *I know this attitude stinks, but I really don't want to sit with Mavis. Not for the whole long ride to Chicago and back. I mean, then I'd be like, stuck with her. I'd probably have to room with her, too. It's not that I don't like her, but . . .* For some reason, Nicole's cruel crack about a 'dork outreach program' echoed in Rockett's brain.

"Atten-*shun*! Up off the floor, ladies — line up for dodgeball."

The sound of the gym teacher's voice struck terror in Rockett. Not because she suffered from dodgeball-phobia. It could have been any teacher's voice. For it suddenly hit her, like a dodgeball to the stomach: If she didn't have a seatmate soon, and if there happened to be an odd number of kids, she might be stuck having to sit next to a teacher on the bus! As Sharla had pointed out, that would be a fate totally worse than death.

So, Arrow or Mavis — who would it be?

Rockett never made a decision that period — she just couldn't, yet.

At the end of the day, the prospect of sitting alone still hanging over her head, Rockett was fiddling with her locker. All at once, she heard a teasing voice behind her, followed by a light tap on the shoulder. "Hey, new girl, all revved up for that art-*rageous* stained-glass window exhibit at the museum? I bet."

Rockett spun around. Trying hard to contain the blush spreading on her cheeks, she countered, "Hey your-self, Ruben — gee, I wouldn't have guessed *you* even knew that much about what's in the museum."

That was my comeback? I think I just beat my own record on the lame-o-meter.

Thankfully, Ruben didn't seem to think it was that bad. His eyes twinkled — and he went with it. "Don't think I'm cultured in an artsy kind of way, huh? You have a lot to learn about me, *chica*."

He still wants to hang out and talk? Awesome! Now I'll do better.

She did. "Well, you have a lot to learn about me, too. I totally want to see the stained-glass thing, but it's the photography exhibit that's first on my list."

Ruben mimed taking a picture. "Click! How could I forget? You're picture-girl — shutterbug-in-chief for the student calendar."

"And the yearbook," Rockett reminded him. "I'm taking my camera along to capture some class trip moments for the yearbook, in fact."

Ruben arched his eyebrows. "Planning to take pictures of us when we least expect it — like on *Gotcha! Camera?*"

He is so totally flirting! I can do this.

Rockett grinned. "Maybe. It depends on what people are doing — but mostly, I just want to capture our class on an awesome trip." She paused. "So what are you most psyched about?"

"In life? Or for the trip?"

He's good. Okay, watch — I can be good, too.

Rockett rolled her eyes. "I've gotta catch the bus, so I don't have time for an essay answer. I meant for the trip — which you so knew."

Ruben's grin widened.

She shoots, she scores!

"Makes no difference what I see, as long as we click *Go!* I'm all about the road. Getting out of here, no parents, no classes, no fear . . . like *Road Rules: The Whistling Pines Episodes!*"

With that, Ruben took a step toward his locker.

Which prompted Rockett to ask, "Bringing your guitar?"

Over his shoulder, Ruben replied, "Like your camera, *chica*, it's part of me. It'll be right next to me on the bus."

That's when it hit her. An idea started to form. And

grow. So large that at that moment there was little room in her brain for anything else.

Which is what compelled her, in the school bus line a few minutes later, to cut in and tap Wolf DuBois on the shoulder.

Turning around slowly, the tall, lanky boy with the bronze complexion smiled down at her, and Rockett — really looking at him for the first time ever — now totally got Nicole's crush on him. He was interesting-looking. But it wasn't him Rockett was interested in.

"Hey, Rockett, what's shakin'?" Wolf asked. "Want to schedule my photo session?"

"Your photo . . . ?" For a split second, Rockett was perplexed.

Wolf seemed amused. He mimicked her announcement in class: "January: Wolf DuBois."

Rockett blushed. "Oh, *that*! Sure. Absolutely. But hey, listen, Wolf. I was just wondering . . ." And then she totally fumbled. "Um, would you happen to know who Ruben is sitting with on the trip? I mean, on the bus ride? That is, are you guys sitting together?"

Could that have come out any more uncool? Lucky for Rockett, the bus pulled up, so maybe Wolf didn't notice the humongo-stupido smile plastered all over her face when he shrugged and answered, "Don't think so. We haven't talked about it. As far as I know, Rosales is solo."

Should I really do this? Ask Ruben to sit with me? As friends, of course. Hello! But . . . mmmm . . . maybe better not. What if he says no way, or worse, laughs at me or something? Can you spell pathetic? I should probably hurry up and ask Arrow or Mavis, before anyone else does. But what if this is an opportunity to hang with Ruben, and I let it go by . . . ? Wouldn't that be even more pathetic?

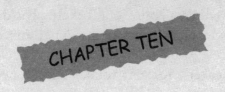
CHAPTER TEN

"Take the window seat, *chica*, I need to sit on the aisle." Probably the glint in Ruben's eye should have tipped Rockett off to his . . . uh . . . agenda. Or maybe she should have remembered his comment about *Road Rules: The Whistling Pines Episodes*. But Rockett was oblivious. She was still tingling from the upshot of the decision she'd made — okay, after lots of should I/shouldn't I obsessing — to call Ruben and ask him to sit with her. It had only taken him a half-second to respond: "You got it, new girl, meetcha on the bus."

Except he almost didn't.

On Friday morning, it seemed the entire eighth grade had arrived at school early and lined up to board the bus. That is, the entire eighth grade minus one. Rockett felt a flurry of panic as she kept checking the line. *Where is he? What if he doesn't show? What if he's sick? Or realized he doesn't want to sit with me and decided not to come? Could this be happening?*

But just as Mr. Baldus blared, "Time to hop on board, eighth-grade class-trippers!" a car pulled up, driven by one of Ruben's older brothers — and out he slithered, not looking nervous at all. Or weighed down. Aside from his guitar case, he was toting only a small backpack.

That was the opposite of Rockett, who'd lugged a backpack, tote, and zipper-busting duffel stuffed with all the necessities. Aside from several changes of clothes and platform sneakers, Rockett totally needed her camera, film, extra batteries, a sketch pad, pens, pencils, chokers, Discman, CDs, toiletries, and accessories.

Her baggage was the first thing Ruben remarked on as he caught up with her, boarding the bus. "Wassup with all that stuff? Planning on moving into the museum?"

Her relief at finally seeing him was mixed with anger at his tardiness *and* his quasi put-down. "I'm planning on getting something out of this trip, for your information — you know, like educational? And recording it for the yearbook, and . . ."

Defensive much? That was a totally stupid way to start this trip!

Not that he heard her. Ruben's attention had already been diverted by Max, who flung a yo-yo at him the minute they were on the bus. Ruben broke out into a huge grin. He stopped short and swung into the aisle seat behind Max. That's when he'd turned to Rockett and advised her to take the window seat, since he'd be "needing" the aisle.

She didn't mind. At least Ruben helped her hoist her duffel into the overhead rack. Plus, she got a chance to survey her classmates as they single-filed it onto the bus. To a one, spirits seemed higher than the Sears Tower. And Rockett's were right up there, with a rooftop view.

Cool! We're right in the middle. This is way better than

90

being stuck in the back. And I totally wouldn't have wanted to be in front by the teachers. I can talk to everyone from here. Even though I think Max might get Ruben into trouble, this is going to rock!

As if to punctuate, Jessie waved at Rockett as she and Darnetta slid into the seat across the aisle from Max and his seatmate, Cleve. "Hey, Rockett," Jessie said, "at least we're sitting near each other. This is good."

"Excellent," Rockett agreed, with a kind of satisfied smile. *Especially now that you see who I'm sitting next to — after you turned me down.*

"Students! Take your seats quickly — the sooner everyone's seat-belted in, the sooner we can get this show on the road." Mr. Rarebit, Rockett's art teacher, called out from the front of the bus. He and Mr. Baldus had volunteered to chaperone along with Principal Herrera and Ms. Chen, the computer science teacher.

In spite of Mr. Rarebit's announcement, Nicole and Stephanie took the most time getting settled, changing their seats several times. Eventually, The Ones decided on the seat diagonally behind Rockett and Ruben. *Too close for comfort!*

But then Nakili and Sharla got on and sat right behind her, which kind of made up for it. Rockett immediately spun around. "Sharla! I'm psyched you decided to come. You won't regret it."

Anticipating a Sharla-snarl, Rockett instinctively flinched — but there was really no reason to. For it seemed as if Sharla had deleted the "mean" from her usual demeanor. Eyes cast out the window, she shrugged. "I figured, why not? What've I got to lose?"

Nakili elbowed her good-naturedly. "Attitude adjustment, girlfriend. Not, what've you got to lose? It's, what's up to gain? Correct response: everything!"

Just then, Miko and Dana, heading to the seat behind Nakili, stopped short. Miko instantly whipped out her camera and instructed, "Okay, first picture. Put your heads together, you two."

As if they'd been buds forever, Nakili and Sharla tilted their heads together — Miko snapped away.

Rockett marveled. *It's got to be Nakili. That girl will win the Nobel Peace Prize some day. She just brings out everyone's good side — even Dana is, like, all-accepting, mellowgirl today.*

As if reading Rockett's mind, Dana reached into her backpack and proffered a bag of bite-size caramel clusters, announcing, "I feel a snack-attack coming on — anyone want?"

Miko arched her eyebrows and pointed to her watch. "It's ten o'clock in the morning, Dana — isn't it a little early for candy?"

With mock seriousness, Dana teased, "Dare to rebel, Miko! It's only ten o'clock in the real world. It's Friday, we're *out* of school — in our own world. We make our own rules."

Sharla was with it. She reached over and dug into the bag. "Caramel clusters, breakfast of champions."

Dana added, "I knew you and I had something in common!"

They do? So I must've dreamed that Dana called Sharla an outcast — and Sharla challenged her to a fight? What's up with this?

Rockett didn't have a lot of time to ponder that enigma, because by then, the bus had filled up and the noise level was approaching a deafening roar. It seemed as if the kids in the other eighth-grade homerooms were mostly in the front of the bus, while hers had snagged the middle section.

Wolf, who ended up sitting next to Bo Pezanski, had grabbed the seat directly across the aisle from her — placing them right in front of Nicole and Stephanie. A proximity that probably made Nicole a happy camper. As did the fact that Nic's other best bud, Whitney — with Viva — was right behind Her-high-and-mighty self.

The back of the bus was staked out by Chaz and Arnold, who were sitting together, and Mavis — who was alone. Rockett made a vow to include her whenever she could.

"Settle down, students! I have some announcements!" Mrs. Herrera positioned herself in the aisle in front of the bus, just as they pulled away from the school. That in itself set the students cheering. "We're off!" "Chicago or bust!" And of course, "*Road Rules*! We rock!"

"I repeat, settle down and give me your full attention," Mrs. Herrera commanded, this time more forcefully — and successfully. The bus quieted.

"Thank you! Let me start by officially welcoming each and every one of you to Whistling Pines' eighth-grade class trip to Chicago — I'm pleased that you all elected to come. I know we're going to spend a most educational weekend together . . ." She paused, then broke out into a smile. "And, I assure you, we're going to have a lot of fun as well."

Mr. Rarebit, from his seat next to her, leaned over and broke in, "As you kids would say, this trip will rock."

Instantly, groans filled the bus — Rockett's among them. *Why is it that when adults try to do our expressions, it always sounds so lame?*

Mrs. Herrera cleared her throat. "Yes, that's it exactly. As I was saying, I have a few announcements. First, this trip will take a long time. While we are on the bus . . ."

"Nicole will check her makeup obsessively!"

That was Max, to whom Nicole instantly retorted, "And Max will display his pathetic attempt to 'show us the funny.' Only, as always, he'll tank!" For effect, she yawned.

For some reason, that seemed to set Arnold off. From the back of the bus, he interjected, "And in that time, Whitney will whine, 'Are we there yet?' ad nauseam."

Whitney, fully annoyed at being dissed by . . . Arnold, grimaced and shouted, "And speaking of nauseam — Arnold will make it totally clear why he is the poster boy for Yuck."

Mrs. Herrera shushed them. "People! If you don't stop

your bickering, you won't hear what we've got planned. Believe me — you will want to!"

Over the next fifteen minutes, the principal sketched out the trip — starting with their arrival. "When we get to the hotel, we'll check into our rooms, and immediately leave for an orientation tour of the city. Then we have a special dinner planned — at a sports-themed restaurant . . ."

"Whoo-*hoo*! A sports place!" Not much got Cleve so pumped that he dropped his cool demeanor — but *that* qualified, as he and several other jocks whooped their approval.

*Dis*approval came from Wolf. The usually quiet boy scoffed, "A sports place? The food will be substandard there."

Before Mrs. Herrera regained control of the group, Cleve shot back, "Just because your parents own a restaurant doesn't make you the expert!"

Wolf's "Any idiot knows that sports and decent grub don't mix" was drowned out by the assist Mr. Baldus gave to Mrs. Herrera. He mimicked a buzzer. "Interruption time is up! From now on, your attention is not requested, it's required!"

Mrs. Herrera took it from there. "As I was saying, after dinner . . . it's back to the hotel, where lights out will be promptly at ten. Tomorrow we've got a full day planned at The Art Institute of Chicago."

Mrs. Herrera then described the rest of their weekend.

Saturday night, they'd go to the Whirligig comedy club. Sunday morning was free-choice: They'd break up into groups, each with a chaperone, and pick an activity. Choices included a visit to the Sears Tower, in-line skating along the waterfront, a Loop sculpture tour, to include Wrigley Field, or shopping. Sunday afternoon, they'd board the bus for home.

It was after the teacher announcements that Rockett learned her first lesson of the trip: *Sitting* with Ruben was a far, far cry from *being* with Ruben. Lesson number two: Her sorta crush had this really, really mischievous side. It wasn't his most attractive angle.

Soon after Mrs. Herrera sat down, Ruben and Max resumed their yo-yo competition. First Ruben Rocked the Cradle. Max did an Eiffel Tower. Then Ruben said, "Look, I made this one up." And he proceeded to do this really involved series of moves he called The Rage.

"That's bogus!" Max retorted. "That's not even a trick. Watch this!" That's when, trying to one-up Ruben, he lost control and flung the yo-yo at Ruben's head.

It was the yelp as the yo-yo connected with Ruben's left ear that brought Mr. Rarebit stomping up the aisle, demanding, "Give me the yo-yos. Now."

Compliance was mandatory — but that didn't stop what Rockett started to think of as "The Ruben and Max Show" from continuing. And it didn't stop other kids from getting in on the fun. A paper airplane glided from Max to Ruben, only it landed in Sharla's hair. Which — at any other time — would have sent her into a scary snit. But not today. She stuck a chewed-up gum ball in it, and zoomed it back to Max, who laughed gleefully.

"Nice one, Norvell!"

Sharla glowed — even as Miko shot her a disapproving look.

Ruben then grabbed it and sent it flying at Cleve, who promptly crumpled it up. But not because he was afraid of reprisals. Cleve had a "better" idea. Reaching under his seat and into his athletic bag, he took out a medium-size inflatable beach ball, blew air into it, and gave it a *thwack!* He aimed at Stephanie, but missed. Wolf tapped it next. He tried to send it to Ruben, but Nicole, who — as predicted — had been checking her makeup, intercepted.

Though Nicole had most probably meant to send it back to Wolf, the ball wafted in Jessie's direction, who immediately joined the game. Deliberately, Jessie sent it flying toward Max. He got it — and tapped it right back at her.

Rockett waved at Jessie. "Send it here!"

Whether Jessie was about to, Rockett would never know. The so-far nonjoiner Bo unexpectedly leaned over and smacked it away from her — zooming it to the back of the bus. Maybe he meant to include Arnold, with whom he'd actually partnered for the class election. Only, Bo's ball ended up hitting Mavis.

Who, head down because she was writing something, was caught completely unaware.

As the ball bounced off her glasses, she screamed in

97

surprise. "Stop it! You made me mess up what I was writing!"

Inwardly, Rockett groaned. *Okay, Mavis could have taken this as a way to be included. I mean, it's an air-filled beach ball, it couldn't hurt anyone. Instead, she goes off on us. And that, Mavis, is why you're in the back, sitting alone.*

Instantly, Rockett felt a sharp stab of guilt about that thought.

Whatever. Mavis's scream had done its damage. This time, it was Ms. Chen's turn at discipline. Teetering on not-made-for-a-moving-bus heels, she gamely marched back and confiscated the ball. Luckily, the usually good-natured teacher wasn't angry. Sighing, she said, "That's enough. You children are going to force us to punish you. And that's not the way we want this trip to go. So come on, let's show how mature you can be."

Maybe because she'd been so nice about it, everyone did calm down. Rockett thought she'd get to talk to Ruben. But before she could say anything, he ended up engaged in an intense burping contest with Wolf. Ick!

Meanwhile, Max leaned over to talk to Jessie.

Rockett was about to turn around and talk to Nakili, but she and Sharla had their backs turned — they'd started a card game with Miko and Dana. Rockett looked out the window. *This is so not what I thought this bus ride would be like.*

I wish I'd never asked Ruben to sit with me! What a baby he is! Sitting with Mavis would have been better.

Rockett watched as mileage on the highway signs to

Chicago got lower. She dozed. The sound of Mrs. Herrera's voice woke her up.

"Well, students. We're about an hour away. So as to avoid any more chaos when we get there, here's what we'll do. First, I'm going to give you some rules. At the hotel, there will be no making phone calls, no watching movies — and no ordering room service. Now we'll pass out paper, onto which you will write three choices of who you want to room with at the hotel. We will do our best to see that everyone get his or her choices."

As Rockett chewed the end of her pencil, deciding who to put down, Ruben tapped her on the shoulder. *Finally — he wants to talk to me!*

But Ruben only had one word for her — "Here" — as he passed her a note.

It was from Jessie. "Write down me and Darnetta and we'll put you. At least that way we'll get to spend some time together."

Could Jessie be any more transparent? She's obviously trying to make up to me for the seat thing — and her big mouth. It's not that I don't want to be her friend again — I really do! — but if I room with them, I'll end up feeling like a third wheel. Still, I should make the effort to get back with her. Or I could put the CSGs. Miko said we'd room together — before the whole Sharla thing. Now they'll probably ask for a quad with Sharla, which will leave me out. The nice thing to do would be to write Mavis — I mean, who else would pick her? But where's the fun then?

Confession Session

Please let me room with Rockett. I've got to talk to her! Not just to apologize for the Max thing — but I need her help. For the "free time" choice, all I need to do is choose shopping and do the thing I've been waiting to do for, like, months! I can't even tell Darnetta. Even though she's the coolest, I have the feeling she might not approve. Rockett will understand, and totally help me.

My plan is going to work so smoothly! I'll just slip away and do the thing I've been planning. All I need to do is separate from the pack, just for a while. I'm sure Steph and Whit will cover for me. BTW: What did I ever see in Wolf? Ugh!

Tomorrow is THE DAY! I feel it in my jawbone, buzzing like a wire of electricity. All I have to do is make myself like a small invisible ghost — which shouldn't be too hard in this crowd. Unless RM decides to cross my intentions, which she better not! If only I am not forced to room with her!

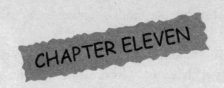

CHAPTER ELEVEN

Several hours after they'd left Whistling Pines, their bus pulled into Chicago. Looking out the window, Rockett marveled at the skyline as the late afternoon sun glinted off the high-rise buildings. She pulled her camera out, already captioning the picture in her mind: "First impressions."

Although they had to put up with Nicole, Max, and Cleve, who claimed bragging rights for having been there before, everyone seemed to be mesmerized by the city. Rockett even forgot about the roommate angst.

But as they filed off the bus and into the lobby of the hotel, her trepidation returned. Mr. Baldus and Mr. Rarebit huddled with the boys, giving out roommate assignments. Principal Herrera and Ms. Chen gathered the girls.

At the last moment, Rockett had finally written down her roomie choices, and now she listened to Mrs. Herrera read off the girl groupings for her friends. She crossed her fingers.

"In Room 604, it will be Whitney, Viva, Arrow, and Ginger," their principal announced. Judging from the high fives of those girls, Rockett guessed that Whitney and Viva really must have bonded on the bus ride. She wondered who Nicole and Stephanie would end up with. . . .

. . . And she couldn't have been more surprised when the answer swiftly came: "Room 606 will be shared by Nicole, Stephanie, Jessie, and Darnetta."

Jessie, distraught, spun around to stare at Rockett. The look on her face made it clear — she knew the truth. Rockett had not requested her.

Well, what did she expect? I mean . . . it's not that I'm still mad at her. Not that much, anyway. If she weren't with Darnetta, it might be different.

"Those are the quads. Now for our trios," Mrs. Herrera said. "In Room 608, we have Nakili, Sharla . . ." Rockett crossed her fingers, hoping for her name. ". . . And Mavis."

Mavis? How'd that happen? But as the words formed in her brain, Rockett knew the answer. Nakili was determined not to leave anyone out. She'd no doubt made a strong case in her request for Mavis to be with her and Sharla. She'd probably urged Sharla to write the same thing.

Dryly, Dana called out, "By process of elimination, that leaves me, Miko . . . and her" — Dana pointed at Rockett — "for Room 610."

Mrs. Herrera nodded. "It's heartening to know you didn't leave your math skills at Whistling Pines, Dana."

Rockett exhaled. *One out of two isn't bad. I did write down Miko along with Nakili and Sharla. At least I'm in with the CSGs, not stuck with The Ones, or worse. I'll just make*

*it my business to get along with Dana, that's all. It's only one
weekend — how hard could it be?*

As soon as they got to their room, Rockett suggested
Dana take the bed by the window, and Miko the one
next to it. That left the small roll-away cot, which Rockett immediately tossed her duffel on.

"You sure?" Dana didn't mask her surprise.

"No big," Rockett replied. "It's just for a couple of
days."

Miko ventured, "We can switch after the first night."

But Rockett assured them she'd be fine.

Then Dana mentioned that both Rockett and Miko
could borrow her hair dryer. As they unpacked, she also
suggested that they all share clothes for the weekend.
"That way we'll have a bigger choice of what to wear."

"Cool idea, Dana," Rockett agreed, feeling totally up.

Then Dana added slyly, "Here's another: Let's have a
slumber party tonight. We'll get Nakili and Sharla and
some of the others to come in, hit the vending machines
for sodas and snacks, and watch movies all night!"

Rockett's eyes widened, but Miko replied first, "Forget
it. Mrs. Herrera said no dice to any of that — and, lights
out at ten, remember?"

Dana's eyes twinkled. "Who's gonna know? The
teachers are on another floor — or was I the only one
who heard that little tidbit? So they'd only find out if
someone told, right?"

Miko frowned. "But the rules . . ."

105

"This is our trip," Dana insisted. "We're away from home, away from our parents and pesty brothers and sisters. We deserve to bust loose and have a little fun. It's not like we're destroying property or hurting someone. Loosen up, Miko — like I said before, we can make our own rules!"

Later, Rockett would wonder if Dana had e-mailed that message to everyone besides herself and Miko. For after the city orientation tour and dinner at the sports restaurant — which, despite Wolf's protests, really was cool and souvenir-worthy — the real "fun" began. Starting with the lights-out-by-ten rule. Yeah, right. After the first of several teacher checks, the curfew went right out the sixth-floor window.

Ruben — no surprise to Rockett by now — turned out to be the ringleader. His mischievous spirit was in hyperdrive. Aided and abetted by his uncharacteristically giddy roommate, Wolf, he seemed determined to break every rule set by the teachers. He made a game of dashing through the sixth-floor hallway, tossing ice cubes like Frisbees, knocking on doors — and calling out, "Room service," to anyone who answered — then running away.

When they knocked on Rockett's door, they actually *had* a room service tray with them, courtesy of Wolf, who — "for research purposes" — ordered a dozen different desserts.

Dana's eyes lit up as she dived into a chocolate confection, while Rockett couldn't resist a strawberry tart. Only Miko refused to partake. "What happens when the bill comes? Then the teachers will know that you broke the rules!"

Wolf's dark eyes twinkled. "I paid for it with the generous spending money we all got for the trip — thanks, Rockett!"

Rockett would have frowned — only her mouth was full of glazed strawberries. Dana, glowing, high-fived him.

When the tray was empty, Wolf checked his watch. "You know, this has been a blast, but the Wolf-man needs to prowl. Who's for blowing this place and checking out the streets of Chicago?"

"You can't do that!" Miko shouted. "It's dangerous. I'd . . . I'd . . . *have* to tell on you."

As if he didn't even hear Miko, Ruben raved, "I have a kickin' idea! Let's live *la vida loca*, set off the fire alarm, and clear the joint out — that way we escape undetected!"

This time Rockett jumped up, superseding even Miko. "Don't you dare!!"

Ruben regarded her with a mixture of curiosity and annoyance. He held his hands up, surrendering. "Down, *chica*! Kidding . . . kidding."

But Rockett was annoyed. "How was I supposed to know that, Ruben? You've been totally immature this whole trip."

She immediately regretted saying that. Especially

107

when he teased, "Excuse me, Mrs. Herrera-with-training-wheels! I'll be a good boy from now on. Please don't give me detention!"

Dana guffawed. Even Miko couldn't stop her amusement from showing.

Rockett wasn't sure why, but Wolf rescued her — and she was grateful. "Cease and desist, dude. Don't put her down. She's about having fun — right, Rockett? She's just into protecting you from crossing the line. Setting off the fire alarm? Bad plan, my man!"

But Ruben shook his head, clearly ticked.

Rockett folded her arms across her chest and stared Ruben down. *He's annoyed at me? Well . . . well . . . vice versa! What did I ever see in him, anyway?*

Finally, Wolf said, "Let's bounce. Enough damage done for one night, bro."

With that, Ruben and Wolf — who left the tray — bolted out the door.

When the phone rang a few moments later, Rockett had the random thought that it was Ruben . . . apologizing.

Not even. The voice on the other end was female — and flustered.

"Rockett — I need to see you. Now!"

Jessie.

Rockett sighed. "Come on over, then. It's not like anyone's asleep here."

"No . . . this is kinda private. Meet me in the hallway, by the ice machine."

As if anticipating Rockett's next question, Jessie added, "It's just between me and you. No one else."

The sight of Jessie in her jammies suddenly reminded Rockett of the slumber parties the girls had shared. She felt a twinge of regret. *I wish we weren't at odds.*

If Jessie felt the same way, she didn't say. Instead, the pj-clad pixie remarked, "You must be having fun. You're still dressed."

Rockett sighed. "I'm not sure I'd call it fun. It's been an eventful day — and night. Anyway, what's up, Jess?" She couldn't stop herself from tossing in, "Problems with 'Netta?"

Jessie made a face. "Come on, Rockett, don't go there. I know that's the reason you didn't ask to room with me. Right? Unless you're still mad about the Max thing. I mean, I know I never really apologized for that. . . ."

Rockett held her hand up. "I'm over it. The Max thing, that is."

Jessie brightened. "You are? How come you never told me?"

I would have — had you bothered to change your plans and sit with me.

She didn't say that, though. Instead, she shrugged. "Didn't get a chance. Anyway, you're right about one thing. I didn't write you down for a roommate, because I feel like a third wheel, Jess — you know?"

Jessie sighed. "I know. I keep trying to get you guys to like each other, but it never seems to work. I don't know, maybe you just need more time. Anyway — this isn't about that. I just found out some stuff — and I wanted you to know."

"What kind of stuff?"

Jessie caught her breath. "I just found out a secret about someone — which I haven't told anyone. Except you."

"You sure you want to?"

"Of course!" Jessie's voice tingled with excitement. "So get this. Nicole is planning on sneaking away from the group, probably tomorrow!"

"She told you?" Rockett could not wrap her brain around Nicole confiding in Jessie. Everyone knew that Nicole thought Jessie was a total dork.

Jessie laughed. "Right. You know she'd never do that! Actually, Stephanie told me, when Nicole and Whitney — oh, did you know this? — they snuck down to the indoor pool, and then to the sauna. Way after lights-out, too!"

"Tell me something surprising. Anyway, so where's Nicole going?"

"I don't know for sure . . . but I think she's meeting someone — who's definitely not with our group."

"Really? Who?"

"That's the thing. It's so secret, she didn't even tell Stephanie! She just said something about keeping a very important appointment."

"Interesting," Rockett mused.

Jessie's eyes twinkled mischievously. "Should we bust her? Tell the teachers? Make up for her telling the whole school about Sharla? 'Cause you know, Max only told Cleve. And okay, so Cleve told her — but *she* spread it around the whole school. Just to make you feel rotten."

Rockett felt a headache coming on. *Rat on Nicole, huh? That's an interesting thought.* She was about to say yes, when Ruben's "Mrs. Herrera-with-training-wheels" taunt came boomeranging at her.

She shook her head. "You know what, Jess? I'm through meddling. Let 'I can get away with anything' girl just try it. She'll get into trouble all by herself."

Jessie grimaced, disappointed. "It's your call, Rockett."

Rockett arched her eyebrows. "You really *do* want to rat her out, don't you?"

"It's not that. Not really. It's more . . . I guess, that I just wanted to make up for the Max thing. I want us to be where we were — close friends again."

"I want that, too, Jessie," Rockett said quietly.

"So are we? Are we there yet?"

Impulsively, Rockett squeezed Jessie's shoulder. "We're on the way, Jessie. Totally."

Relieved, Jessie let out a long sigh. "Um, so there's one more thing. I kinda need you to cover for me on Sunday. . . ."

Rockett listened carefully as Jessie described her plan. Before the girls parted for the night, she'd agreed to help Jessie break one tiny little rule.

* * *

Rockett hadn't been back in her own room five minutes when the door burst open and Nakili came blasting through.

Before anyone could ask what was up, the CSGs leader commanded, "Emergency meeting!"

Dana and Miko hurried over, and the three of them jumped up on the bed and sat cross-legged.

"What's the 911?" Dana asked.

Nakili motioned to Rockett. "This means you, too. Haul tush over here, girlfriend. This time, *I* need advice. From all of you."

She's including me! Cool! But I wonder where Sharla is. . . .

As if she could read Rockett's mind, Nakili said, "I made Sharla stay back with Mavis. And I didn't tell her what I just found out."

"Spill!" Dana demanded.

Nakili caught her breath. "Mavis has a secret plan. It's a doozy — and it's dangerous."

Dana, instantly *un*impressed, sniffed, "Gee, what could it be? Is bizarro-seer girl planning to foretell the next great Chicago fire? Or the Cubs winning the pennant?"

Nakili waved her away. "This is serious, y'all. Mavis is planning to meet someone. A stranger she met . . . in a chat room, on-line."

Above Miko's gasp of horror, Dana demanded, "And you know this exactly how?"

"Well, you know how she's been writing all during the trip? She kinda left her notebook open on my bed. I wasn't going to look at it, but she caught me holding it and assumed I already had. So she just got all defensive. While I was trying to explain that I didn't look at it, the truth came out."

Rockett's jaw dropped. "But Mavis knows better than to try and find someone she met on-line."

Nakili exhaled. "You'd think. But it's a boy. And he lives in Chicago — that's what he said. And she's feeling like this might be her only chance to meet him. So she's plotting to separate from the group tomorrow and hook up in some part of the museum we're not going to."

"That's dangerous! We *have* to tell a teacher." Miko folded her arms across her chest.

"Wait." Nakili slowed down. "It's not like I didn't try to talk her out of it. But I struck out. I thought about telling a teacher. But there's more."

"Hello, what else could there be? Mavis shouldn't even be talking on-line with someone she doesn't know." Miko was strident now.

Nakili ignored her. "But here's the deal, y'all. This guy — he's definitely in junior high school, like us. He told her about his classes, and they're almost on the same curriculum and all. They even compared answers to tests. They connect. See, he represents himself as being all spiritual and stuff. They talk about how neither one of them is accepted in school. And how they both believe in the spirit world, stuff like that."

"Even so, how can she know it's not some random poseur?" Dana asked. "Or does her sick sense . . . ha-ha, *sixth* sense, tell her it's a guy?"

Nakili answered, "She showed me the e-mails."

"She printed them out?" Dana asked, getting into it now.

"I saw them," Nakili answered. "And they are really sweet. Anyway, the thing is, to Mavis, she's finally met someone who . . . well, who doesn't think she's weird. In her head, this is the first boy who's gotten to know the real her. And she sees this as her big chance to meet him. There's nothing anyone can say that's going to discourage her. And, on the real, maybe we shouldn't try to stop her."

That was it. Miko jumped off the bed, shrieking, "Nakili! I can't believe I'm hearing you say this. Mavis could be meeting a random person! I say, 'No way!'"

Nakili sucked her breath in. She looked at Dana. "What do you say?"

Dana shrugged. "I think you're right. Let the little nerd have her moment of acceptance."

Nakili considered. "What about this? What about if one of us . . . follows her . . . to this secret meeting. Just hangs out of sight, makes sure she's not in any danger. She doesn't have to know. We'd just be protecting her, is all. And she'll meet her cyber crush — if it *is* a cyber crush." Nakili turned to Rockett. "You're a friend of Mavis's. What's your feeling?"

Before Rockett could respond, Dana reminded them

harshly, "We don't need her vote to decide what to do. She's not a CSG. It's two against one. We let Mavis have her meeting. And if you insist, we shadow her."

Oh! My! God! I just figured it out. What if — could this really be? — it turns out that the person Mavis is meeting is . . . Nicole? Like Jessie said, she's sneaking away to meet someone, too. It would be just like Nicole to know it's Mavis and play this kind of a cruel joke on her.

I can't let that happen! I mean, it's bad enough that I didn't sit with her, and she's all alone in the back of the bus. And, even though she doesn't know it, I totally didn't put her down to room with. Maybe I don't want to hang out with her, but I don't want to see her hurt and humiliated — especially by Her Nastiness, Nicole! I so know what that feels like! Should I say something to the CSGs?

While Rockett weighed her options, Dana said, "Well, that's decided." Nakili nodded. "Okay, then. The three of us will shadow her tomorrow. That's it."

I'm glad I didn't say anything to them. Dana couldn't stay friendly for more than an hour. She just had to remind everyone how part of their group I'm not! I should tell Jessie. But . . . okay, I know I shouldn't think this way, but then what if she tells Max? Who tells Nicole again. Then Mavis would really be hurt. But who else can I ask? Maybe . . . nah . . . Sharla? Maybe she secretly sympathizes with Mavis and would understand how horrible it would be if Nicole is playing an evil trick on Mavis?

"I'm gonna get some ice."

Before Nakili, Miko, or Dana could react, Rockett abruptly left the room. Only she didn't head to the ice machine. Instead, she marched down the hall and rapped loudly on Room 608.

Sharla answered. "Checking up on me, Movado? Guess I'm busted. 'Cause it's way past ten, and as you can see, the lights are on!"

Rockett ignored the sarcasm. Instead, she glanced around Sharla to see where Mavis was — sitting up in bed, under the covers, writing.

She caught her breath. "Sharla, can I see you for a minute, in private?"

Sharla yawned, but nodded and called over her shoulder, "Yo, wavy Mavie . . . I'm outta here. Don't do anything I wouldn't! Ha!"

Mavis barely reacted. "Shush, I'm busy."

Quickly, Rockett led Sharla down the hall and ducked into the vending machine alcove.

Though she tried not to show it, Sharla couldn't hide her curiosity. "So, RoMo, how'd I get to be confidential-girl? Still on the outs with Jessie?"

Irritated, Rockett retorted, "For your information, Jessie and I are five by five. And stop calling me RoMo."

Sharla folded her arms. "So whatcha need me for?"

"Okay, this is kind of a situation . . . well, I just think you're the best person to talk to. I mean that."

Sharla softened. "Yap away, then."

In a rush, Rockett described what she'd just found out. Nicole's sneak-away scheme — possibly to meet someone. Worse, Mavis's plan to definitely meet someone.

Sharla threw her head back, snickering. "*That's* what you're obsessing about? Let me get this straight. You think Nicole's been playing an evil joke on Mavis, pretending to be her cyber admirer, only to make Chicago humiliation-station?"

Rockett nodded. "I can't let that happen!"

"Anyone ever tell you you're a gold medalist in conclusion jumping? *I* heard your little friend Jessie's planning on sneaking away, too. And I also happen to know the Wolf-man's got a secret mission. So how come you're not implicating them?"

Rockett sighed. "I know what Jessie's plan is — she's gonna get her ears pierced on Sunday. Her mom doesn't want her to, so she's gonna do it here. As for Wolf, he's probably going restaurant hopping. That's his deal. No, it's not them. It's either Nicole . . . or some stranger."

Sharla considered. "So what's Nakili's plan? I know she's got one, that's why she bolted before. She's all friendly to me, but when it comes to something important, I'm pushed aside — she hobnobs with her real buds."

"You get a lot of things, don't you, Sharla?" Rockett said quietly.

"We outsiders always do."

Rockett felt a stab in her heart. Not just for Sharla. For she knew Sharla meant Mavis, too. Which is what led her to say, "So maybe I'm wrong about the Nicole thing. Maybe Mavis *is* going to meet a guy. And I guess we should let her . . . have a chance at something . . . nice . . . happening. I guess it's possible."

The force of Sharla's blast rocked her. "Are you nuts, Movado? No way! Say for some strange reason you're actually right this time. Which, segue, would go down in history. But say you are. Say Nicole has been putting her on all this time — pretending to be some guy who likes her. And Mavis finds out when they 'meet.' Devastation-city."

"But we still don't *know* it's Nicole. We could be wrong. I guess."

Sharla rolled her eyes. "Do you always make that beeping noise when you back up, RoMo? Let's discuss amongst ourselves. Didn't you say it's probably a kid because they have, like, the same subjects in school? Some random person wouldn't be able to go over test answers with her! And some random person wouldn't know all Mavis's peculiarities and pretend to, like, take them seriously. Hence, it's probably someone from our very own beloved Whistling Pines!"

Rockett mused, "But, what about this? What if it is Nicole . . . only she doesn't know it's Mavis. I mean . . . what if, like, Nicole's different when she's e-mailing someone she doesn't know. What if she has, like, this secret nice side that she shares . . . ?"

She trailed off. Simultaneously, Rockett and Sharla shook their heads. "Nah."

Sharla finished. "If it's Nicole, trust me — and trust your first instinct — she knows it's Mavis. And wouldn't it be just like Nicole to stroke her own ego by making someone else feel like a loser?"

"Completely in character," Rockett agreed with a sigh.

Sharla continued. "So if you really care about saving the Mave, it's simple. Just make sure that face-time doesn't happen. And for extra credit, you'll have foiled nasty Nicole's nefarious scheme!"

Rockett couldn't stifle a giggle. "You have an amazing way with words, Sharla. Who knew?"

Mea culpa alert. No one in the school bothered to get to know Sharla. Covering, Rockett said, "But how can I prevent them from meeting?"

Sharla shrugged. "How? You're the Rockett-girl, you're large and in charge — figure it out."

Impulsively, Rockett touched Sharla's arm. "Help me?"

119

Although Sharla recoiled slightly, a barely perceptible smile played on her lips. "Deal, Camille, but just straight up — we keep Mave from her cyber crave."

"Thanks, Sharla. I owe you one," Rockett said sincerely.

Sharla shot back, "No, Movado. You owe me two. Like I forgot what you did to me back at school? I don't think so."

When Rockett got back to her room, Dana pounced. "Where's the ice?"

Rockett reacted quickly. "Changed my mind."

"Gong! Wrong answer. You never intended to get any. Not taking the ice bucket was the giveaway."

Rockett sighed. "Okay, you win. I took a walk to think about Mavis. And anyway" — she hoped she sounded convincing — "Nakili was right. I am her . . . well, friend in a way."

Before Dana could remind her that she "didn't have a vote" in what the CSGs were going to do, Rockett rushed on. "So how about *I* shadow her? I'll just make it my business to accidentally-on-purpose be wherever she is — even in the girls' room and stuff like that. That way, you three won't miss seeing any of the cool stuff in the museum. You won't be distracted playing bodyguard to Mavis."

Miko rushed over and gave her a hug. "That is soooo totally nice of you, Rockett. Are you sure? I mean, can you handle it?"

"If I can't, I'll call for backup."

Dana threw her a shrug. "Looks like the me-so-selfless Rockett is ready for takeoff. What's in it for you — except your compulsion to meddle?"

Nakili was bugged — at Dana. "End of story. Just say 'Thank you, Rockett.'"

The next morning, on the bus to the museum, Mr. Rarebit explained their assignment. "Because we have only one day in the museum, you must get the most out of it. We've printed up a list of the top twenty exhibits. Each of you will chose a total of ten to concentrate on — no fewer. Your assignment, when we get back to school, will be to describe what each piece of art said to you — and then tell us which had the most impact on you, and why."

For a split second, Rockett panicked. *What if the Mavis caper keeps me from seeing the photography exhibit? How choice would that be?*

But the next thing she heard lifted her spirits. As Mr. Rarebit handed out the list of exhibits, he continued, "Because traveling together in one large group will be too unwieldy, each of you will buddy up with one other person whose interests most closely match yours. That way, you can explore the museum in twos, and spend more time at specific exhibits."

Instantly, Rockett exchanged a knowing glance with Sharla. The teacher had just handed them a plan. They'd pair up, then trail Mavis and her partner all day. Not just

121

to shadow her — as had been the CSGs' plan — but to intervene, make sure Mavis never got to ditch her buddy and meet up with her on-line "friend."

A few minutes later, Mr. Rarebit walked down the aisle of the bus, making sure everyone had a buddy. Rockett watched carefully to see who Nicole had chosen and, naturally, who Mavis would be with for the day. She crossed her fingers.

Rockett cringed at the Nicole-Stephanie pairing. *Stephanie! The girl most likely to let Nicole do whatever she pleases, no matter what. In fact, Stephanie will probably come along for the let's-humiliate-Mavis ride!*

Mr. Rarebit allowed a Ruben-Wolf matchup — though he warned them to behave, and okayed Cleve and Max, plus Chaz and Bo. When he got to the back of the bus, Rockett prayed, *Let Mavis end up with a teacher! An adult would never let her out of her sight. Let Mavis pair up with anyone but . . .*

". . . Arnold Zeitbaum."

Mr. Rarebit's acknowledgment that Arnold would partner with Mavis stunned Rockett. *Mavis and Arnold? How did that happen? Those two can't stand the sight of each other!*

But soon Rockett realized exactly why they'd chosen to buddy up. No doubt Arnold had no one else — and, most definitely, neither was likely to mind losing sight of the other: Mavis especially! All she had to do was tell Arnold she was hitting the girls' room. He'd never wait around for her. And she'd be free.

But when? It occurred to Rockett that Mavis had probably already set a time.

Just then the bus came to a stop. Rockett, fretting, hardly realized they'd arrived. And then she looked out the window for her first glimpse of the Art Institute. She gasped. There, right in front of her, were the famous brass lions that flanked the museum's main entrance. And it hit her. We're really here! I can't believe it — this is mega-major!

As the Whistling Pines group filed up the stairs into the museum, Rockett and Sharla wasted no time. They positioned themselves right behind Mavis and Arnold. Which is what led them first to the exhibit that would never have made Rockett's list in a million years. Some snore-worthy arms and armor collection.

There, behind huge display cases and hanging on the gallery walls, were authentic suits of armor and archival weapons like swords and daggers, preserved from the fifteenth century.

Arnold was practically salivating as his eyes darted all over the room. "I am awed — finally, in the presence of greatness and beauty!" he intoned, to no one in particular, as he took copious notes.

Rockett half expected someone to quip, "No, we're in the presence of great boring-ness." Only no one did.

Mavis instead seemed to be taking notes, pausing every now and then to check her watch. After a while, she turned to Rockett. "Funny, you never mentioned you were interested in this. Not in all the time I've known you."

For a split second, Rockett panicked. Smoothly, Sharla saved her. "Who said *she's* interested? I am. And to make up for what she did to me in school, she's agreed to be my buddy. And do everything I want."

Sharla elbowed Rockett, probably a little harder than necessary. "Isn't that right, RoMo?"

"That's it . . . exactly."

Mavis shrugged and turned to Arnold. "Come on, Lancelot, we have to get to ten of these exhibits. Let's go on."

But Arnold was far from finished. "Go to the next exhibit. I'll meet you."

Rockett reacted swiftly. "You can't. The teachers said stay together."

Mavis rolled her eyes and walked over to a bench against the wall. "I've got some writing to do anyway. Let the medieval moron get his fill. You two can leave."

But Sharla nixed that. "Not so fast. I didn't take notes on that neat-o bow. You never know when that'll come up on a quiz!"

Finally, after what seemed like forever, Arnold was ready to move on. So far, Mavis hadn't objected to Rockett and Sharla's presence. And the usually strong-willed Mavis didn't seem to mind Arnold leading the way.

He chose to view Grant Wood's *American Gothic* next, the way-famous painting of a serious-looking, pitchfork-clutching farmer and his daughter. It turned out to be a popular choice with the Whistling Pines crew. Rockett counted Jessie and Darnetta, Wolf, Ruben, Max, and Cleve all scribbling notes about it.

Exception: Max and Ruben weren't writing. They were mimicking the painting's pose — which totally cracked everyone up.

Mavis wasn't amused. "I hate this painting! I read about it. It shows how these two can't tolerate anything different from their narrow little beliefs."

Wolf added thoughtfully, "I read that, too, but I'm not so sure it's true. There's good in them. You can see that no matter what hardships they've faced, they're still all about the land . . . just like many Native Americans."

Ruben scratched his head. "Man, all this is getting way too deep for me. C'mon, let's go. I see on this list that they salvaged the trading room of the old Chicago Stock Exchange here somewhere. At least that's about moolah — a primo interest of mine!" He rubbed his hands together.

Rockett caught that and rocked back on her heels. *Ruben's into money? I'm finding out all sorts of info I didn't know. I'm not sure how I feel about that.*

It wasn't until they'd made their way into another gallery that Mavis began to bristle at Rockett's presence. As Arnold gazed reverently at a famous painting, Mavis focused on Rockett and Sharla. "Don't you two have something else to see? I mean, why are you still with us?"

Sharla shrugged. "Coincidence, I guess."

Mavis scowled but said nothing.

Sharla pointed at the painting. "Didn't this dude chop his ear off or something?"

"He was a tortured soul," Arnold said quietly, and Sharla nodded.

They're . . . bonding? I'm getting weirded out!

Suddenly, Mavis turned and started to walk away.

Panicked, Rockett yelled, "Where are you going?"

Mavis frowned. "Do I need permission to go to the ladies' room, Rockett?"

The bathroom! This is it! She's going to ditch Arnold. And us . . . and go meet up with . . . Nicole.

"I'm going with you," Rockett said decisively.

Mavis made a face. "Why?"

"You're supposed to stay with your buddy, anyway, and Arnold obviously can't come."

"Get a grip, Rockett. You're taking this buddy thing too seriously."

Rockett shrugged. "I have to go anyway. We'll be right back, you guys."

Sharla waved her away. "Take your time. There's so much to absorb here."

Rockett had been wrong. Mavis wasn't trying to sneak off.

That didn't happen until much later.

After lunch in the cafeteria and a trip through the Impressionist galleries, Mavis began to seem totally nervous — and openly resentful of her "shadows."

126

As they strolled through the museum, Arnold announced, "This next one's for you, Rockett. We'll go see the photography galleries."

Mavis whirled around. "This one's for *her*? What are you talking about, you dodo bird? She's not even supposed to be with us."

Before Arnold could retort, Sharla piped up, "Get over it, Mave, looks like all four of us have similar interests. I mean, who'da thunk it?"

Mavis seethed. "Stop calling me that! In school, we have nothing in common. You never speak to me. Or anyone."

Sharla shrugged. "Sometimes it takes a change of scenery. And speaking of scenery, check this baby out." She pointed up the stairway. It was dominated by a humongous painting.

Rockett gasped. "Wow! I can't believe how big this is. It's . . . it's . . ."

Just then, she heard Nakili's voice. "Inspiring. Serene. Magical."

Rockett spun around. "Celestial."

As Dana stepped forward to get a better look, Nakili tapped Rockett's elbow and whispered, "Anything happening? Do you need us?"

"Not yet," Rockett replied under her breath. "And we've only got another hour or so here . . . maybe we were wrong?"

Nakili crossed her fingers. "Keep hope alive."

* * *

Rockett felt almost optimistic by the time they reached the photography galleries. She knew they housed some of the earliest photographs ever taken, plus classic shots by modern photographers. Mr. Rarebit had mentioned that if she was really passionate about pictures, she'd get a lot out of studying their work. He was right — she immediately became engrossed.

Which is why she didn't notice her quarry start to slink away. Mavis appeared to be enthralled by a particular photograph: which just happened to be situated by the alcove leading to other parts of the museum.

Sharla kicked Rockett's sneaker. "Don't look now, but our Mavie's on the move."

Rockett jerked around — but didn't immediately see the danger. "She's looking at that picture, taking notes. I don't think so."

"Trust me, Movado. I know the body language of someone who's about to bolt. Done it myself . . . on more than one occasion."

Reluctantly, Rockett turned from the photo she'd been taking notes on. But when Mavis still hadn't moved for a couple of minutes, she started to turn back.

Sharla reminded her, "Mission abandoned?"

"Not even! But look, she's not going anywhere . . ." Just as the words left her lips, Mavis swiftly turned — and bolted through the alcove.

"After her!" Rockett and Sharla plowed through the crowd, headed for the alcove.

Arnold, confused, spun around. "Where are you going?" he shouted.

Rockett yelled over her shoulder, "We have to stop Mavis!"

"Stop her from what?" Because Arnold's question went unanswered, he decided to find out for himself. He bolted after the girls.

He saw Rockett and Sharla scurrying down the hallway — only to stop in their tracks when they came to a choice of corridors to go down. Rockett shouted, "Did you see which way she went?"

Sharla, out of breath, shook her head.

Arnold caught up with them. "What happened? You're acting like crazy Mavis escaped from the loony bin."

Rockett had no time for explanations. "Look, Arnold, we just need to find her — okay? Either help us or get out of the way."

Arnold was unaccustomed to Rockett's take-charge tone. "Sorry! I didn't know the situation was so dire."

Rockett commanded, "Head down this corridor — to the right."

"What do I do if I find her?" he asked.

Sharla barked. "Just grab her and bring her back to this spot. Do not let her interact with another human being, no matter who it is! Got that?"

Arnold lit up. "A mission! I will carry it out! Godspeed!" He dashed down the hallway.

Sharla motioned to the left. "I'll take this one. We'll meet back here."

Rockett raced straight down the hallway, the paintings on the wall becoming one huge blur.

I can't believe I'm not getting to spend any time here! How'd I get myself into this mess, anyway?

"Miss! Slow down! There's no running in the gallery!" a guard admonished her, and planted himself in her path.

"Sorry — this is an emer . . ." Rockett started to explain, but just then, she spotted her. Mavis had just turned the corner into another room.

Rockett threw the guard her most apologetic smile. "I just found the person I was looking for." She speed-walked into the room Mavis had just disappeared into.

Luck was with her. The room was fairly empty and Mavis was still alone.

"Mavis!" Rockett cried out, finally catching up with her.

Mavis whirled around, shocked and annoyed. "Go away, Rockett!"

But Rockett grasped her elbow. "I can't. I mean, you've got to come with me. Back to where Arnold is."

Mavis took Rockett's hand off her. "I will be right back — I just need to see something. By myself."

"But it's against the rules."

"Rockett Movado, you're not the boss of me!"

"Come on, Mavis, wandering off by yourself, you could get lost. Or worse."

Mavis glanced furtively around the room. "I can read the signs, Rockett. I won't get lost. Now . . . just . . . scram! I need my private space."

Rockett started to panic. "I can't let you, Mavis. I need you to come back with me. Now."

Mavis checked her watch. Little beads of sweat appeared on her forehead. "Please, Rockett, I just need you to leave. I can't tell you why, you'll just have to trust me. Which, if you were a real friend, you would."

"I am a real friend, Mavis. Which is why I can't."

The two faced off: equally determined.

Just then, a familiar voice wafted into the room. "Wassup, art-girl *chicas?*"

Ruben?

Rockett spun around. He and Wolf sauntered in.

Yes! For once your timing is aces, Ruben. No way will Mavis hang out and meet her cyber admirer with all of us here. You just saved the day!

Rockett acted like they were long-lost friends. "How's it going, you guys? Did you see everything you wanted?"

Wolf scratched his head and looked around. "Uh,

131

pretty much. But I . . . we only hit nine exhibits so far. Guess we'll count this as our last." He gestured around the room.

Rockett nodded and furtively glanced around for anything she could recognize. "This is an unbelievable exhibit. Look at this stone carving! And this sculpture! You wandered into the best spot. Didn't he, Mavis?"

But her frazzled friend was scowling.

And then she stomped away.

"What's up with her?" Rockett heard Ruben ask, as she rushed to catch up with Mavis — who scurried into the nearest ladies' room.

Rockett got there just in time to find Mavis awash in tears. And Rockett felt a sudden and unexpected wave of empathy. "Mavis . . . I'm . . . please don't cry. It's better this way."

Mavis looked up. "It's better, Rockett? Like you know?"

It was when Mavis started to shake violently that Rockett knew she had to offer some explanation for what she just did.

Motioning to a bench, Rockett ventured, "Mavis . . . um . . . sit down, okay?"

Mavis, shaking and sobbing, allowed herself to be led. She dropped her notepad on the floor.

Rockett stooped to pick it up. *Should I tell her what I know? What I suspect?*

She didn't have to. Mavis's sixth sense was in hyperdrive. Or maybe it was just common sense. But she already knew.

"I shouldn't have told Nakili!" Mavis wailed. "But she snooped in my secret journal — so I had to explain. I can't believe, of all people, she told you — meddlesome Movado, the one person who would do an act of aggression to try to stop me."

Rockett fished in her bag for some tissues and handed them to Mavis.

"I was trying to protect you, Mavis."

"Protect me from what? From meeting someone who's really cool — not superficially, but deep down? Thanks, Rockett, that's exactly the kind of protection I don't need!"

Softly, Rockett tried to make her point. "I know you think it's a guy. A guy our age, who's totally worthy. I wish that were true, Mavis, I really do."

"How do you know it isn't?" Mavis demanded. "It's me with the psychic awareness, not you, Rockett!"

"It's just that on-line, people can pretend to be who they're not. And I . . ."

Suddenly, Mavis dipped into her bag and extracted a batch of paper, which she'd tied with a red ribbon. "Read these," she commanded. "And then you'll see. No phony wrote these. He is real. And he likes me, Rockett — he likes me for who I am. He wouldn't care that, you know, I might not be the most popular person around school. He gets me."

Rockett began to read the e-mails that Mavis had, just like Nakili said, printed out. They were all signed by a WA.One.U@yippee.com.

Rockett sucked in her breath. The use of "One" in the person's name made her surer than ever it was Nicole — *W* was probably for Whittaker, and Rockett knew Nicole's middle name was Anne.

Mavis's cyber name was Seer2000.

Deer Seer2000,

I, too, sometimes feel like a loner in a mixed-up, crazy school full of snobs. All they care about is how they look. If I talked about other things, like the spirit world or mystical experiences, I know they'd laugh at me.

Deer Seer2000,

I've never met anyone like you. You are truly an alternative thinker, but you are on the side of all things good. I know this. I wish we could meet.

Rockett bowed her head. *It's possible these could be from a cool guy. But it's also possible they could still be from a weirdo . . . or worse, from Nicole. Maybe she's letting down her snob-guard, or maybe she knows it's Mavis and is toying with her. Either way, I did the right thing. Only Mavis will never believe that.*

"These are pretty huge, Mavis, but they still don't prove . . ."

Mavis wasn't listening. She grabbed the letters away from Rockett and shook her head. "He is my soul mate. And this was my one chance to meet him. And because of you, now I won't. Your betrayal is really ironic, Rockett."

"I wasn't trying to betray you, Mavis. That's the last thing I would do. I just . . . why is it ironic, anyway?"

Mavis blew her nose. And suddenly she laughed. Only it came out more like a bitter cackle.

"It's ironic because if it weren't for you, I wouldn't even be on this trip."

And that's when it all sank in.

Hoarsely, Rockett whispered, "The note! That anonymous note I got back at school — the person thanking me was you! And the person crying in the bathroom that day, it wasn't Sharla. It was . . . you. I don't know what to say."

"There's nothing to say. Actions speak louder and yours spoke volumes. Maybe you don't know this, Rockett, but since my mother left, it's just my father. He's a scientist and sometimes scientists aren't exactly rolling in dough. So I wouldn't have been able to come if not for your fund-raising plan. But the only reason I needed to come was to meet . . . him. And you took that chance away from me. From this day forward, Rockett, I am not your friend."

Rockett hadn't noticed Sharla slip into the ladies' room. Until she heard that familiar voice. "No good deed goes unpunished. Typical."

I should just tell her that I was afraid she'd be meeting some crazy person — and leave it at that. No. I have to tell her the truth — that it's Nicole. Then she'd understand why I did what I did. But what if we were all wrong, and I really did keep Mavis from meeting her . . . soul mate. Talk about ironic — this time Dana would've been right.

CHAPTER FOURTEEN

Rockett could tell that Chicago's Whirligig comedy troupe was kicking funny-bone butt — everyone around her was laughing. But she sat there, at a table with Jessie and Darnetta, grim-faced.

Nakili, Dana, Miko, Sharla, and Mavis were sitting together at a table pretty far away. Rockett was sure Mavis chose it.

She'd decided, finally, *not* to tell Mavis the reason she'd acted as she did, so only Sharla knew the real story of what had gone down at the museum earlier in the day. Her other friends could see that Rockett had landed on planet Glum, but didn't know why.

Jessie didn't need the full 411 to try and cheer up Rockett. She whispered through the skits — just in case Rockett just didn't get the jokes. During intermission, while Darnetta went to get the snacks, Jessie accelerated her efforts. "Did you get to the Egyptian hall at the museum?"

Rockett shook her head.

"It was so awesome! I was totally face-to-face with an actual mummy case . . . hey, that rhymes! Anyway, I can't wait to tell my mom. And I bought these amazing scarab earrings. . . ."

When still Rockett didn't react, Jessie plowed on, "The photography exhibit rocked, too. I looked for you there, but I guess you must have gone earlier. Is that what you're gonna use for your report?"

"Probably." Rockett sighed. She'd barely managed more than a few minutes in that wing. But she wouldn't tell Jessie why. She was relieved, in fact, when they were interrupted by Nakili. Ignoring Jessie, she said, "Come talk to me for a sec."

Reluctantly, Rockett got up and followed Nakili to a corner of the room.

Nakili pointed at her. "Ever since we got back from the museum, you've been acting weird. And now you're acting like we're at the Whirligig Tragedy Troupe. So what's up — did something go down with Mavis you're not saying?"

Rockett shrugged. "I told you, she never met up with anyone."

"I get that. *She's* in pity-city. What's *your* excuse?"

Miko came up behind Nakili. She ventured, "Is it because you missed all the stuff you wanted to see? I feel so bad about that, Rockett. I'll share all my notes with you. And I got all these postcards and souvenirs at the gift shop. You're, like, welcome to anything you want."

Rockett had to smile. "It's okay, Miko, thanks anyway. I got to see . . . you know, some stuff."

Miko pressed on. "You did a good thing, Rockett. It'll come back to you."

Rockett squirmed. "Uh, speaking of coming back, I better go sit down. Intermission's almost over. Probably."

But just before the second act started, one more friend buzzed by Rockett's table. "Experiencing extreme glumness, new girl?" Ruben balanced a tray of pop on the palm of one hand and shot her a friendly look. "I can lend an ear. Or a pop. Or . . . I can go back to the snack stand and get something else for you. . . ."

At that moment, there was no sign of clown-boy, just the cool, sincere kid she'd liked from day one. But she shook her head. "No thanks, Ruben. I'm not real hungry, or thirsty."

"Later, then." He slipped into his seat just as the lights dimmed.

Every so often during the show, Rockett glanced over at The Ones — just like in the school cafeteria, Nicole, Stephanie, Max, Cleve, and Chaz sat together. Whitney was with them, too, even though she'd spent most of the trip hanging with Arrow, Viva, and Ginger.

Rockett focused on Nicole. The haughty One alternated between cracking up at the skits and rolling her eyes. Her cyber meeting never happened. So was she chagrined at not getting the chance to humiliate Mavis?

On Sunday, for their free-time morning, Rockett went shopping with a group that included Jessie, Nicole, Stephanie, Max, Cleve, and Chaz. Three hours at the Galleria Mall wouldn't have been Rockett's first choice — in-line skating with Arrow and Whitney along Lakeshore Drive was way more appealing — but she'd promised Jessie. In the end, though, she was glad she'd gone, partly because Darnetta had opted for the Sears Tower tour.

Ms. Chen was their chaperone. "As long as you stay in twos, and check in every hour, you're free to explore the mall," she'd told the group.

Rockett and Jessie's first stop: a jewelry store that offered free ear piercing with the purchase of a pair of gold-plated studs.

"I'm so pumped!" Jessie exclaimed as she sat in the chair, clutching the side armrest.

"You're . . . um . . . sure?" Rockett asked. "Your mom won't kill you?"

"Totally. But she'll forgive me. Eventually . . . ouch!" Jessie jumped a little at the first prick of the needle.

The woman doing the piercing looked up. "Sorry, it's not supposed to hurt. Do you want to continue?"

Jessie grimaced, but nodded. "It's okay. I was just nervous."

And a half hour later, the proud new owner of gold-plated stud earrings was thrilled. She stopped at every mirror they passed, exclaiming, "I love my new look! I can't wait to wear my new scarab earrings! What do you think?"

"It kicks, Jessie."

Jessie regarded her. "Thanks for coming with me and, you know, being supportive."

Rockett shrugged. "Sure."

Jessie furrowed her brow. "It's just that, well . . . 'Netta's the best and all, but I'm not so sure she would have gone along with me on this."

Rockett arched her eyebrows.

"She's kind of weird about that, you know, she might have been more like, 'Your mother said no, so don't do it,'" Jessie rushed on. "Anyway, I still want you two to be friends, but I'm superglad you're here."

Rockett couldn't hide a smile. "I'm glad, too, Jessie."

"Okay! We did the thing I wanted to accomplish — tag, you're it. What do you want to buy?"

"I hadn't really thought about it," Rockett replied honestly.

"Well, then I'll do the thinking for both of us," Jessie said with a gleam in her eye. "After all, we've got to spend the money we raised!"

Over the next several hours, Jessie managed to lift Rockett out of the doldrums. They picked up plaid platform sneakers. And a nail tattoo kit. "We'll do matching temporary lady-bug tattoos," Jessie squealed when she spied them.

At hourly intervals, Rockett and Jessie checked in with Ms. Chen. So did the others in their group. The first time, Nicole breezed by, swinging several shopping bags from designer boutiques.

Ms. Chen frowned. "Nicole, you were only supposed to spend the money you were given. Not more. This already seems over the limit."

Nicole shot her a sly smile. "I can't help it if I'm an expert shopper. I get a lot of bang for my buck."

Ms. Chen looked unconvinced. "Watch it."

At the second check-in, Nicole had added to her shopping bag cache by two more. But it wasn't until the appointed time to go back to the bus that Ms. Chen, the picture of calm all through the trip, went ballistic: Nicole and Stephanie didn't show up. The group waited an extra twenty minutes. Then their teacher called security and had the girls paged.

A few minutes later, the two appeared. But instead of being apologetic, Nicole and Stephanie acted completely carefree.

Ms. Chen, while reprimanding them harshly for their tardy, didn't comment on the surplus of shopping bags Nicole now toted.

In spite of Ruben's sweetness at the comedy show, Rockett almost wished she could pick a new seatmate for the long ride home. But that wasn't going to happen. Because of Nicole and Stephanie, her group was the last to board the bus. And everyone was already in the seats they'd had going there.

The Ones were in a clutch behind and opposite her. Nakili, Sharla, Miko, and Dana were directly behind her, Mavis and Arnold in the way back. The former museum buddies were back to not speaking — at least not to each other.

Arnold was in high spirits, chatting up anyone who'd listen all about his inspiring day. Mavis had pushed the mute button. She didn't return Rockett's smile or wave.

Rockett slipped into the window seat next to Ruben. She braced for the worst: a rewind of asinine antics. But nuh-*uh*. This time he and his buds seemed mischief-depleted. The mood, in fact, was pretty mellow all around.

Only Nicole kept up a steady, high-pitched banter. Accompanied by the incessant rustling of tissue-paper-stuffed shopping bags, she displayed and described her purchases to anyone interested. Mostly that included Stephanie and Whitney, whose impressed squeals fed Nicole's ego.

It also brought Ms. Chen, after a while, to the back of the bus. Frowning, she pointed at Nicole. "I guess your tardiness wasn't enough. It also seems you've broken the spending rule — and now are busy bragging about it."

Nicole's first tactic was denial. "No way. Like I told you, I'm just an expert shopper."

"Is that so?" Ms. Chen arched her eyebrows. "In that case, you won't mind if I look at the receipts . . . for everything you bought?"

Nicole next went with girlish giggles. "Well, okay, maybe I overdid it just a smidge, but Ms. C, you of all people will totally appreciate the incredible bargains I got. Anyone can see how chic you are. I just bet you're a smart shopper, too."

Swing and a miss. Ms. Chen crossed her arms. "Don't

try to butter me up, I'm not a baked potato. What I am is disappointed in you, Nicole. We'll be talking detention when we get back."

Nicole seethed. "Detention! How unfair is that? Just because I broke some retro rule that we never should have had . . ."

Loudly, Ms. Chen repeated, "With detention, as you know, comes the possibility of relinquishing your role as president of the student body."

Nicole, rabid now, whirled around and pointed at Rockett. "If it weren't for her, the do-good bully, this wouldn't even be an issue!"

That last outburst boomeranged on Nicole. It brought Mrs. Herrera storming back. "You're busted, Nicole. End of story. We'll revisit this tomorrow."

Over Nicole's protests, Stephanie's gasps, and Whitney's wail of "Wait, that's not right," Jessie turned around to Rockett and passed her a note.

"So that was her big secret. Stephanie told me the wrong thing. She wasn't going to meet someone — she was meeting lots of someones: designers!"

While Rockett absorbed that, Nicole continued to object to the unfairness of it all. And then she made an impulsive decision: If she was going down, she wasn't going alone.

Peevishly, she said, "I'm not the only one who broke that stupid little rule. Max did, too. He bought silver earrings and a matching necklace, and believe me they were way over the spending limit."

Both teacher chaperones turned to Max, who instantly turned red! Anticipating their wrath, Max stammered, "Hey . . . hey . . . wait! I had an exception to the rule. I had to buy a gift . . . for . . . my . . . mother." He trailed off, "It's her birthday."

He needn't have sweated it. To Nicole, Ms. Chen murmured, "How about you don't rat out your friends? You are the one who's in trouble here. Not only did you break a rule, but you brazenly bragged about it — in front of your teachers? You have only yourself to blame, Nicole."

While Ms. C was reaming out Nicole, Rockett checked out Max. Who stole an embarrassed glance at Jessie.

Was the gift really for Jessie? And if it was, is he too embarrassed to admit it? Maybe he doesn't want her to know he really likes her? No, it's not that. It's . . . oh, I hope I'm wrong, but maybe he doesn't want his snobby friends to know he likes her.

Ruben tapped Rockett on the shoulder. She flinched. He grinned. "Deep thoughts?"

"Not . . . really. You just, I don't know, surprised me or something."

Ruben eyed her curiously. "Look, new girl, you and me haven't been exactly cool with each other this trip . . . but you know I was mostly only kidding, don't you?"

"When you called me Mrs. Herrera-with-training-wheels you were definitely not kidding, Ruben."

"Oh, come on, give a guy a break. It was my first night

away from the 'rents, bustin' out . . . so maybe I got a little *loco*. Forgive me?"

He looked so cute, Rockett wanted to — but he wasn't getting off the hook that easily. "I don't like it when you make me feel I'm ruining your fun. That's all."

Ruben stretched his legs and threw his arms over his head. "That's what's wigged you out, the whole trip?"

Suddenly, Rockett felt tired. "No, that only annoyed me a little. It's just . . . some other stuff happened that I didn't anticipate. And it didn't go so well."

The next thing Ruben said took Rockett by surprise. "I can relate. I'm kinda bummed, too."

"You are? Why?"

Ruben nodded. "Not so much for myself, but my man didn't have a *muy* ragin' time on this trip, and I'm bummed on his account."

Rockett scrunched her nose. "Your man?"

Ruben nodded to the seat across from them. "The Wolf-man. His mission on this junket? Unaccomplished."

"He didn't sneak away to different restaurants?" Rockett guessed.

"Restaurants?" Ruben looked confused. "No, I mean, Wolf likes to check things out and report to his parents, but that wasn't it."

"What didn't he get to do, then?"

Ruben flipped around to see if Wolf was listening, but his partner-in-petty-crime had earplugs on and his eyes closed. He lowered his voice to a whisper. "See, Wolf was angling to meet a cyber sweetie. She stood him up."

The sound Rockett just heard? Her jaw crashing to the floor.

And then she sucked in her breath. "Ruben . . . without breaking anyone's trust, could you give me some back story?"

"His *corazón*, his heart, is what's broken — nothing else to break," Ruben said. And then he told Rockett something she never expected to hear. Nor did she need him to finish the story into it, she knew all this was true.

Nakili had been wrong: It wasn't some random crazy writing to Mavis.

She and Sharla had been right: It was someone in junior high school. *Their* junior high school.

But she, Sharla, and Jessie had gotten the most important clue all wrong: It wasn't Nicole playing a trick on Mavis, and it wasn't Nicole letting her snob-guard down and coming off as a nice person.

Mavis's sixth sense was on target. It *was* a guy. A guy so cool, even Nicole had a crush on him! Mavis would not have gotten hurt; she might even have a friend, an ally at school.

Mavis had been wrong only about one thing. He didn't live in Chicago. And it was Rockett — butting in again! — who stopped the meeting from happening.

Ruben remarked, "You know what this trip is missing?" Without waiting for an answer, he stood up and grabbed his guitar from the overhead shelf. As soon as he started strumming, Nakili leaned over and tapped him on the shoulder. "Can you play 'Friends 4ever'?"

Ruben nodded. "Hip-hop style? Or classic?"

Nakili grinned. "You pick."

His and Nakili's voice were soon joined by others on the bus. For the rest of the trip, Ruben took requests, going through slow, sweet ballads to kickin' rock 'n' roll to cheesy camp songs. The sing-along ended only when the bus pulled up to Whistling Pines Junior High School.

Should I tell Ruben the truth — that it was really Mavis? If I do that, he'll tell Wolf. And then what? What if Wolf is, like, appalled or something? How much worse would that be? Maybe I'll just tell Mavis. But I have no idea if that'll make her feel better or worse. I could ask Sharla what to do — obviously in one way, she relates to Mavis. I could totally tell Jessie. Or . . . on second thought? Maybe not. Maybe I won't tell anyone this time.

Confession Session

Okay, so I blew a wad on a gift for Jessie. But when Nic busted me, I couldn't just blurt it out, could I? What kind of crap would I get from Cleve and Chaz then?

I am so torn! On one hand, this trip was mega-awesome. Rockett and I had a blast at the mall. She totally supported me with the ear thing, which I knew she would. I feel like we are almost totally back together. But, on the other hand — I thought Max was getting a present for me. He *said* he was going to! That's the whole reason I told him what the fundraiser was for. Did he lie to me?

Detention? I don't think so. I'll get out of it somehow.
I'm less bummed than I was, I guess. If it's meant to be, if she's meant to reveal herself to me . . . she will. All in good time. Anyway, the rest of the trip went great. Ruben and I were solid, man. And who can resist seeing Nicole brought down a peg? I mean, the girl's cute, no denying. But she can't touch the sweet soul who's been writing to me.

CHAPTER FIFTEEN

Monday morning, before homeroom, Rockett caught up with Mavis, who was fiddling with her locker. Motioning toward the still empty stairway, Rockett gently asked, "Could I talk to you? In private?"

Mavis shot her a dark look. "What for, Rockett? So you can ruin my life some more?"

Rockett sighed. "I'm so sorry, but . . ."

"Apology not accepted. Just go away."

"I didn't come to apologize. I mean, I *did* . . . totally . . . but there's something important I have to tell you."

"So tell me."

Rockett looked around. The hallway was starting to fill up with kids. "Just give me, like, two minutes. Come to the stairwell, where no one can hear us."

Reluctantly, Mavis trudged after Rockett. "I know what you want, Rockett. To tell me the identity of the boy I wanted to meet."

Rockett blanched. "You know it's . . ."

"What I know," Mavis interrupted, "is that you think *you* know. That's your big reason for dragging me over here."

Rockett gulped. "I'm impressed, Mavis, I really am.

'Cause you're right. And . . . the truth is . . . you were right about everything. I was wrong. I jumped to this conclusion and messed things up for you. But maybe, when I tell you, things can be good. Maybe you can still meet him."

Mavis snorted. "Like I'm getting another chance to go to Chicago any time in this decade? In case you have a memory short circuit, my father and I are not exactly rolling in dough."

Rockett put her hand on Mavis's shoulder. "I haven't forgotten. But I believe things will get better. Anyway, who said anything about you going to Chicago? Maybe there's one thing your sixth sense was a little off about . . . maybe he . . . this person wasn't so honest about where he lived."

"He doesn't live in Chicago?" Mavis squinted behind her thick glasses.

"No, he doesn't. Think about it for one second. There's a reason you were able to compare your subjects and your classes and stuff. . . ."

"He's in junior high," Mavis insisted. "And lots of schools have the same subjects."

"He's in *this* junior high," Rockett said gently.

"No!" The force of Mavis's denial took Rockett by surprise. "There is no boy at Whistling Pines who is as deep, as thoughtful, as spiritual as . . ."

"He is." Rockett pointed to the tall, angular boy who just so happened to be sauntering by at that moment.

And Mavis gasped so loud, Wolf whirled around. He shot her a funny look, but kept on walking.

Mavis turned red. The second Wolf walked away, she pounced on Rockett. "You're deluded! What would give you the dunderheaded idea that WA.One.U is Wolf?"

So Rockett had to tell her. How Wolf had told Ruben, and how Ruben had quoted the e-mails exactly.

"Think about it, Mavis. Even his cyber name. WA is probably Wolf Antler, that's his middle name. And One is for one world. And U, isn't that part of the Pawnee language symbol for Wolf?"

Mavis took it all in. Urgently, she asked, "Does he know it's . . . me?"

"No one does. Your secret's safe. If you want to tell Wolf that you're the girl on the other end of the computer, that's your call. Of course, if you want my opinion, I think you should totally go for it."

Mavis did *so* not agree. To the max. When she regained her composure, she nearly exploded, "No way would I ever tell him! Wolf DuBois? Ugh. He creeps me out!"

Rockett was reeling. "Wha . . . ? How's that even possible?"

Mavis sniffed. "Look at him! He's got raisin-cookie eyes! And that tooth thing he wears around his neck all the time. He gives me the heebie-jeebies."

Rockett refused to accept Mavis's blanket dislike of Wolf — based, as it seemed to be, purely on his looks.

"So you're saying you don't like him just because you think he's funny-looking?"

Mavis folded her arms across her chest. "I have a right to my opinions."

She's judging him by his looks? That's so completely bogus. She of all people should know better.

But Rockett decided not to say that. "Look, you probably know more about him than anyone in the whole school. And you have to admit, in cyberspace there's a lot you liked about him. A lot you had in common. You even talked about being soul mates!"

Mavis shook her head furiously. "I was wrong. No, I never want him to know. Swear to me, Rockett, that this goes no further. You will never tell anyone!"

Rockett put her right hand up. "I promise. Never, ever."

Mavis sighed. "Even though you don't deserve it, I forgive you, Rockett. I probably couldn't have stayed mad at you, for long anyway."

From behind her, a voice snickered, "Lots of people could, though!"

Rockett whirled around. Before she could utter a word, Sharla commanded, "Movado! Girls' room, now!"

What now? She can't be mad at me — I didn't do anything this time!

"Chill, RoMo," Sharla reassured her the minute she closed the door behind them. "I'm not ticked off at you or anything."

"Then what's with the dire tone of voice?"

Sharla shrugged. "I have a rep to keep up. Now that we're back in school."

"Oh, I get it."

"Yeah, well, here. Get this." From out of her backpack, Sharla withdrew a box and thrust it at Rockett.

"What's this?"

"No clues, open it and see."

As soon as she did, Rockett gasped. "Sharla! You shouldn't have!"

"Yeah, I know, but that's my problem, always doing things I shouldn't."

Rockett ran her fingers across the shiny cover of the oversize book, *Photographs from the Permanent Collection of The Art Institute of Chicago*. She began to page through it. "Sharla, this is so amazing. It's exactly what I would have bought . . ."

"If you had time. Yeah, yeah, I know. If you weren't busy meddling in other people's business." Sharla snickered — good-naturedly. "I got it in the gift shop. I know it's not the same as being there, but anyway, it's a souvenir."

"Sharla! This is . . . I don't know what to say."

"Then don't say anything, okay? That's the best thing you could do."

Cradling her book, Rockett slipped into her seat, just under the homeroom tardy bell. As Mr. Baldus took attendance, Ruben leaned over to talk to her. "All recovered from the trip?"

Rockett nodded. "You?" She'd never told him that Mavis was Wolf's secret correspondent. And she never would.

When the bell rang, Ruben fell into step with her, toward first period. "You seem less wigged than you did yesterday. The effects of my serenade on the bus, or a good night's sleep?"

Rockett grinned. "Here's the thing, Ruben. On the trip, I kind of messed up, jumping to conclusions. But in a funny way, things worked out for the best."

"I don't know if you messed up or not, *chica*," he said sincerely. "But I know this. When something's done with a pure heart, things often work out for the best. And even though we butted heads on the trip, one thing I think I can say about you: New girl, you do have a pure heart."

How could one boy be so immature . . . and so wise at the same time?

"So, anyway," Ruben continued, "here's the deal. I heard about this party coming up in a few weeks, and I wanted to be sure you were gonna be there before I commit. You know, I have a lot on my plate."

Rockett lit up. *He is so back to flirting!* "I haven't been invited to any party yet, but if I am, I'll be there. Just promise me something. No yo-yos, no burping contests, no setting off the fire alarm . . ."

"You're taking all the fun out of *la vida loca*!" Then he bit his lip and smiled. "For you, I'll do it! So how 'bout we hang out after school?"

"I can't hang *out*, but you can help me hang something *up* — I have some posters to put up on the school walls and I need to do it this afternoon."

The next day, Rockett found herself surrounded by curious classmates.

Chaz was one of the first. Pointing to one of the posters, he said, "I'm confused. What is this about, Rockett?"

She grinned. "What does it look like, Chaz? It's the times and places for people to come and get their picture taken for the calendar. You still want to be part of it, don't you?"

He bristled. "Of *course* — but riddle me this. Why does it say 'Everyone is welcome to pose'? What happened to the choices you already made?"

"I tossed 'em!" Rockett replied happily. "After last weekend, on our class trip, I had a change of heart — and if I do say so myself, a pretty brilliant idea."

It was a brilliant idea — Rockett's most brilliant, in fact. She had a little help from Mr. Rarebit, Mr. Baldus, Mrs. Herrera, and Ms. Chen. What she'd written on the posters was this:

ATTENTION, EIGHTH GRADERS. PHOTO SESSIONS FOR CALENDAR POSING WILL BE HELD ONSTAGE IN THE AUDITORIUM. EVERYONE IS WELCOME TO POSE! AND HEAR THIS: IF YOU POSE USING SOMETHING YOU LEARNED FROM OUR TRIP, THAT WILL COUNT AS YOUR ART ASSIGNMENT. BE A SCULPTURE! BE A PAINTING! BE CREATIVE!! BE THERE!!

All day long, kids stopped her in the hallway, asking, "What's up with this?" And all day long, Rockett repeated herself. When the CSGs came over, she explained, "It suddenly occurred to me — a little belatedly, but whatever — *why* only one person per month? It's our calendar, we can make our own rules."

She shot Dana a grin as she said that, before adding, "And, big bonus, our teachers agreed that everyone can use the calendar pose as a way to complete the art assignment. Remember, the idea was to do a report on what inspired you, what affected you the most. Instead of writing it, you get to express it artistically."

"That's so much better!" Miko was all for it. So was Nakili. Dana started to demur, just out of habit, but stopped herself. "Nice goin', Rockett."

Which is how, by the end of the following week, Rockett, along with Jessie and fellow photographer Darnetta, found herself in the school's darkroom, poring over the photos. Darnetta had shot the first half, Rockett the second. The girls acted as each other's stylists.

There was Wolf in January: miming the pose of a Mayan carving he'd seen.

For February, Arnold got his wish to pose in a full suit of armor! Rockett didn't even want to know where, exactly, he'd gotten it! Next to him, Jessie — in her scarab earrings, was wrapped up mummy-style.

For March, Darnetta had asked Rockett to photograph only her hands. Rockett was totally impressed with Darnetta's creativity — and lack of ego.

On the other hand, April featured only Cleve, posed like an early trader from the Chicago Stock Exchange.

May, however, ended up as Rockett's favorite. Ruben and Arrow re-created the *American Gothic* painting. Only, in place of the pitchfork, the two proudly held a guitar. When Rockett questioned the choice, Ruben winked. "You know how Mavis and Wolf were talking about this at the museum? Well, I decided that this painting is open to interpretation — just like me!"

The unlikely duo of Ginger and Bo found a common interest for June. They dressed as the subjects in a painting of Paris.

For July, Rockett had actually coordinated with Stephanie to pose like two people in a photograph they'd seen.

Okay, so August turned out to be the most discordant photograph. Chaz chose to pose as a dictator while Nicole, naturally, posed as a princess.

September featured Viva and Sharla, who'd dressed up in 1920s gear.

October was the Max-Whitney-Mavis troika. Even they had found common ground, posing as people on a tropical island. Rockett didn't completely believe that Max and Mavis wanted to do this — but Whitney probably did, and had talked them into it. Whatever — it worked!

Miko had November all to herself and chose to pose holding a replica of an Asian woodblock print.

And, in December, Nakili and Dana had settled on dressing as a couple of young acrobats.

"I just have one question, Rockett," Jessie said, after all the shots were chosen. "Did you come up with a name for the calendar, now that it's kinda different from our original plan?"

"I did, Jessie. I'm actually borrowing Nicole's suggestion and calling it 'The Cool — and Creative — Kids of Whistling Pines Calendar.'"

Jessie arched her eyebrows. "It works, but why?"

"Because, Jessie — here's the real. We're amazingly creative. And we are all cool in our own way."

"Big up to that, Rockett!"

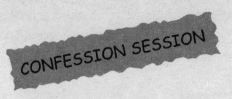
CONFESSION SESSION

ABOUT THE AUTHOR

Lauren Day: Pseudonym-alert! My real name is Randi Reisfeld and I've written lots of books for teens and 'tweens. Maybe you've read some. I've done a bunch in the *Clueless* series (based on the classic movie and TV show); the *Moesha* series; *Meet the Stars of Animorphs*; and *Prince William: The Boy Who Will Be King*, to cite a few that are circa now. Then there's *Got Issues Much? Celebrities Share Their Traumas and Triumphs*, where today's top young stars tell how they got through the tough times. Landing in *Rockett's World* is my coolest writing gig so far — I hope you come along for all the journeys.

Meet me at

www.purple-moon.com

Find out more about these
great CD-ROM titles!

Camp brings new friends and
experiences ... are you ready?

What do dreams mean?